The Mansfield Killings

A novel based on actual events

By Scott Fields

FIRST EDITION
ISBN 10 - 0982993137
ISBN 13 – 978-0-9829931-3-2
eISBN: 978-1-3018323-5-4

December 2012

This book is dedicated to John, Nolana, and Phyllis Niebel, three innocent victims.

Chapter One

The cold steel door rolled across the track and slammed shut with a metallic resonance heard down the corridor. The young man sat on the edge of his cot and fumbled with the buttons on his shirt. As expected, a deep voice boomed, "Lights out," and, immediately, giant switches were tripped throwing the entire east wing into near total darkness. Lighting fixtures with one dimly lit florescent tube were placed every twenty feet providing just enough light for prison guards to keep a watchful eye.

Twenty-four year old Robert Daniels removed his shirt and hung it on a nail. He started to unfasten his belt when he noticed a figure of a man standing in front of his cell. He was a big man with rounded shoulders and long arms. Silhouetted by the dim light behind him, the lone figure had a menacing almost evil look about him.

"Heard you made parole," said the man, his voice deep and solemn.

"Harris?"

"It's still Mr. Harris to you, boy."

"Not after tomorrow."

"Don't get cocky, boy. You're not out of here yet."

Daniels stared at the figure. His jaws tightened, his hands became fists. "I'm gonna get you, Harris," he muttered.

"What did you say?"

Daniels leaned back against the wall running his hands through his hair. He would have to wait. Wait until another time. Wait until the odds were in his favor. However Red Harris would most certainly pay dearly for what he did.

"Nothing," he muttered again.

"That's what I thought," said Harris as he turned and walked away.

It was September 24, 1947. Robert Murl Daniels had served over four years of a one to twenty-five year term in the Ohio State Reformatory in Mansfield, Ohio for robbery committed in Pike County, Ohio. Much to the amazement and genuine concern of the guards and other employees who knew Daniels, he was to be released the following day. In the past, inmates who were granted an early release earned that privilege by leading an exemplary life while incarcerated. They worked on the farm, in the kitchen, at the shoe shop, wherever they could make a contribution while learning a trade as well.

Robert Daniels was different. Admittedly, he worked in various shops during his stay inside. In fact, he was praised for his diligence and fastidious concern for the detail of his work. Most inmates worked at a job inside simply to occupy the long and seemingly endless hours. Daniels took a genuine interest in his work and pridefully displayed his finished wares to the others in his shop. While this was a positive attribute, uncharacteristic of the typical inmate, there was something unmistakably sinister, even evil about this man. Others sensed it.

Some feared him, while others simply avoided any confrontations with the man.

Robert Murl Daniels was five feet, eight inches in height, with a slender build and sandy hair. He was always well-groomed and neatly dressed, usually in a suit and tie. He was considered a ladies' man by all who knew him and was never without female admirers. Despite his short stature, Daniels walked tall and erect with his head held high, described by many as a prideful gait and by others as an arrogant strut. He had a handsome face with a smile that many women considered as seductive. A first impression of the young man would characterize him as an up and coming executive, ambitious and qualified for success instead of the heinous monster that he became.

Daniels was born in Columbus, Ohio in 1924. His was not a happy childhood. It seemed to Daniels that his parents never stopped arguing and fighting. It bothered him as a child and continued to affect his life even after he left home.

Early in his childhood, Daniels suffered a head and spinal injury from a fall out of a kiddy wagon. For months he was unable to move, and this debilitated condition put the boy into what was described as an unconscious state of mind. The injury manifested itself later in lapses of memory.

At the age of 13, Daniels suffered from another head injury while riding on a bike and was unconscious for several days.

Eleven years later, Daniel's lawyer would defend his client in a murder trial by declaring that since those childhood accidents, his acts have been psychopathic and that he has suffered severe headaches, delusions and hallucinations, and lapses of memory.

As a boy, fist fights and altercations became commonplace for the young man. As he progressed into his teen years, the fights and confrontations became more violent with the combatants bloodied sometimes beyond recognition.

In 1941, Daniels was sentenced to the Boys' Industrial School at Lancaster, Ohio for automobile theft.

Then, in 1943, he was sentenced to the Mansfield Reformatory after a conviction on an unarmed robbery charge at Waverly in Southern Ohio. He later escaped from the Grafton honor camp, but gave himself up in Columbus and returned to the Reformatory.

Daniels only served a little over four years of a 25-year sentence. Because of the severity of the crime and the potential danger that Daniels posed, the parole board was severely criticized. Considering their track record, it was difficult to understand why Daniels would be granted a parole when the vast preponderance of inmates facing the board were denied an early release. However, those who knew him well were not surprised. His good looks and charm along with his excellent work record was persuasive enough to influence just about anybody sitting in judgment over him.

The next morning Daniels joined the other inmates in line and marched down to the dining hall as he had every morning for the last four and a half years. However, this morning was different for Daniels. This morning was his last breakfast inside prison walls. In fact, it would be his last meal for his release was set at 11:00 a.m. In just a little over three hours, he would be a free man.

He shuffled through the line and filled his plate with scrambled eggs, sausage and toast. He grabbed a cup of coffee and turned to the dining room. Sure enough, there he was. He was sitting at the third table from the back wall like he did every morning for the past eight months. John Coulter West was his name. He was twenty-two years old and admitted into the Mansfield Reformatory on January 16, 1947 to serve a one to seven year term for grand larceny from Summit County.

Despite their different backgrounds and personalities, West and Daniels became instant friends. Other than lock up, they spent nearly all their time together.

Daniels dropped his tray of food onto the table and sat down across from West.

"Guess who's gettin' out of here in just about three hours?" said Daniels, his face beaming.

West said nothing. He continued to eat his breakfast.

"Johnnie, look at me. I'm getting out of here."

West swallowed a mouthful and looked at Daniels, his hand and fork frozen in mid air. "So, what am I supposed to do about it?"

Daniels leaned over the table until his face was inches from his friend. "You can be happy for me; that's what you can do about it."

West stabbed a hunk of sausage and thrust it in his mouth. "Well, I'm happy for you," he said with a sneer. "Are you happy now?"

"What the hell is your problem?"

"I don't have a problem."

"Yes, you do."

"No, I don't."

"You're acting like a jerk on the most important day of my life," said Daniels. "Now, what's the problem?"

West looked up at Daniels with egg clinging to his lips and chin. "That's just it. You're getting out of here, and I have six years to go. What am I supposed to do in here by myself?"

Daniels glanced around at the crowded room. "Good Lord, you could hardly consider yourself alone in the place."

Just like Daniels, John Coulter West was short. He was thin, almost gaunt, and unlike Daniels, West was not particularly handsome at all. He wore black framed glasses and had an uncommonly large nose. He had a severe case of acne that continued even into his adult life. Those who knew him would guess that he was never happy for he wore a sneer on his face that never went away.

John West, or as Daniels frequently called him, Johnnie, was imprisoned on a charge of grand larceny having stolen four truck tires and rims from the Weaver Trailer and Body Company in Akron. This wasn't the first time he had been in trouble, but it was the first time he had been sentenced. He had previously been on probation for burglary and larceny.

West sipped his coffee. "It won't be the same. They're not my friends."

Daniels reached across the table and wiped the egg from West's chin. "Ah, don't worry about it. Who needs friends anyhow? You'll be out of here in no time. Take me for example. I could have been in here for 25 years, and I'm out in less than five."

"How did you do it anyhow?"

"You need to be the most perfect, ideal inmate. You want them to think of you as a citizen rather than a criminal."

"I've been good."

"Ya gotta be better than good," said Daniels, excitedly flaying his hands in the air. "Get a job in one shop and show them you love to work. That's what good citizens do. Remember, you want them to think of you as a citizen not a criminal."

"I can be a citizen," said West.

"That's the spirit."

"I can be a good citizen."

"That's good, but don't go overboard here."

"Why? Don't you think I can be a good citizen?"

"Johnnie, do you have any idea what we're talking about?"

"Yeah, you said I had to be good."

"Well, it's more than that," said Daniels. "You can't cuss, especially when you use God's name, you can't steal, can't talk back to any of the guards, do what you're told without complaining, work hard in a shop, and, as an added touch, donate your money to some kind of charity."

"Ah, can't I keep my money?"

"Do ya want to get out of here?"

West said nothing. He put down his fork and leaned back in his chair. It was if he was considering the question. "Yeah, I want to get out of here."

Daniels pointed at his chin. "You got egg on your face again. Wipe it off."

West rubbed his face, and the food dropped onto his shirt.

Daniels leaned over the table. "Now listen up," he said with a voice nearly a whisper. West moved closer. "When you get out of here, you come look me up at the address I wrote down for you. You and I are going to make some serious money."

West shook his head. "I ain't workin' no job."

"I'm not talking about work. I want to rob stores. That's what I'm talking about."

West smiled. "That's what I hoped you would say."

Daniels leaned closer, his voice even softer. He stared into West's eyes. "Lean over here a little closer."

West could tell that something was wrong. Never had he seen such an evil look on anybody's face.

"You and I are making a pact right here and now," said Daniels, his jaw tightening even more. "Let's you and I vow that someday soon we'll come back here to Mansfield and settle up with Red Harris."

West smiled, exposing his discolored, crooked teeth. "I like that idea."

Daniels' eyebrows furrowed. "He has to pay for all the beatings he gave us."

He thrust out his hand, and West grabbed it with a smile. "If it's the last thing we do," said West.

"I gotta go see the warden," said Daniels getting to his feet. He pointed at West. "Now don't forget our pact, you hear?"

"I won't."

Daniels walked away. "Take care, my friend."

West watched his friend walk across the room and disappear through a doorway. He was alone again, and he didn't like it. It seemed like he was always alone, all his life. Daniels was the only real friend he had ever known.

John Coulter West was born in Parkersburg, West Virginia. Shortly after he was born, his parents separated and eventually divorced. Years later, in a drunken stupor, his father told him that he was the reason for their divorce. West never forgot what his father said, and actually carried the guilt to his grave.

After the separation, West lived with his mother, and thus began his life of living alone. She worked sixty to seventy hours a week as a waitress in a diner. He learned at an early age how to cook his own meals and was expected to clean up after himself. If she came home from work and the dishes were not washed, she would scream at him and threaten to kick him out of the house. West never doubted her word. He always believed and feared that one day she would do just that. She had a quick temper, and even at an early age, West recognized and respected her fits of anger. One evening, his mother came home to find that West had forgotten to wash a frying pan. He had not used it. In fact, she had fried eggs for herself that morning and had left it on the stove. She screamed at West and accused him of being lazy and thoughtless. Her ranting of anger escalated until she grabbed him and threw him out the door. It was early fall, and as the sun slowly disappeared over the rooftops, the evening air quickly cooled. West huddled next to the backdoor hoping that she would soon come to her senses and let him back inside. By morning, the temperature had dropped to just under thirty degrees. West's shivering was near convulsions when his mother finally opened the door to let him in. She apologized to him but declared that experience would serve as a warning to a young boy who didn't do as he was told.

Unlike Daniels, who had a higher than average Intelligence Quotient, West had an I.Q. of 60, which legally categorized him as a moron. Since he was inherently quiet and stoic by nature, his lack of intelligence was not obvious. However, it was painfully obvious to the other children in school. He was woefully behind all the others in all subjects, and his classmates maliciously pointed it out with every opportunity. After repeating the first grade for the third time and with the advice of his mother, West dropped out of school. His mother would not allow him to stay at home, so, at the tender age of nine, he was told to find a job. His search was fruitless for the first two months, until a bar owner, in desperate need, hired him to wash dishes. It was there that he acquired a taste for alcohol, and by the time he was twelve, he was already an alcoholic.

West's life of crime had its roots in the taverns where he worked. Most of the meager salary that he earned was turned over to his mother for his share of the household expenses. With the paltry amount of money left over, he could ill afford the expensive gins and bourbons for which he had acquired a taste. He discovered that it was remarkably easy to slip bottles from the backroom and set them outside for a later time after work when he would pick them up. His life of crime was interrupted one day when the tavern owner was waiting for him after work.

Luckily for West, the owner didn't turn him in, but he did lose his job. It was shortly after that incident that West began to realize that if he was going to risk going to jail, it might as well be for something worth more than a bottle of gin.

Unfortunately for West, he wasn't skilled, adept or even had the promise of a future in crime. He successfully pulled off two robberies before he was caught and put on probation. The next offense landed him a sentence that brought him to the Mansfield Reformatory.

Mansfield's Reformatory, with its medieval exterior was considered one of Ohio's greatest buildings, when it opened on September 15, 1896, at a cost of 1.3 million dollars, it was America's largest reformatory. This massive building resembled an Old World gothic castle and had the world's largest freestanding cellblock standing six tiers high.

In 1861, long before the grounds would become a reformatory and then a prison, Civil War soldiers used the area as a training camp, Camp Mordecai Bartley it was called. The camp was named in honor of a Mansfield man who served as governor in the 1840s.

The site was officially voted as the candidate for the construction of a new Intermediate Penitentiary in 1867. The intention of The Intermediate was to serve as a mid-point or a go between for the Boys Industrial School in Lancaster and the State Penitentiary in Columbus. First-time offenders, most of which were quite young, would receive a chance to be reformed.

Construction began in 1885, when head architect, Levi T. Scott laid out blue prints of his design, which was supposedly in the style of a Cathedral. It was generally thought that the design should instill a feeling of hope in the inmates, to inspire them to develop into better human beings. What it eventually wound up resembling was Count Dracula's castle.

Daniel's meeting with the warden was concluded after less than an hour. As was the formality for any inmate reentering society as a parolee, there were certain irrevocable guidelines that must be followed or he would be returned to the reformatory to finish his sentence. Daniels shook the warden's hand and started down the hallway. For the first time since being confined to this institution, Robert Daniels had a smile on his face. After all, in another two hours, he would be free, free to walk any street; free to eat in any restaurant he wanted. Daniels vowed that he would never again take his freedom for granted.

As he turned the corner and started down another corridor, the door to a broom closet opened blocking his path. A hand reached out, grabbed him by the shirt, and dragged him inside. Daniels struggled to get free, but someone had a vise-like grip on him.

He finally broke free and turned to face his aggressor. It was Red Harris. Harris took the blunt end of a policeman's nightstick and jabbed it into Daniel's stomach. He buckled in pain. Harris then rapped him on the back sending him head first into the wall.

"You know I was always careful not to leave any marks or bruises on you," said Harris. "Your word against mine, kinda thing. Well, seeing as how you're leaving real soon, I guess it doesn't make much difference, now does it?" Harris grabbed

Daniels by the throat and slammed him against the wall. "Now, get this straight. You come looking for me on the outside; I'll kill you, plain and simple. You got it?" Daniels nodded his head. He eased his grip, and Daniels relaxed. Then, without warning, Harris slammed his knee into Daniels' groin dropping him to the floor.

Harris opened the door and stepped over Daniels, who was writhing in pain. "Take care of yourself," he said with a subtle, yet maddening voice.

Daniels propped himself up with one hand and watched with loathing disgust and anger as Harris walked away.

Chapter Two

Mansfield, Ohio was a small city nestled in the heart of Ohio's sprawling farmlands. Travelers from other states characterized Ohio as that, "flat as a board" state, and if they were traveling on the western half of the state, that would have been an accurate description. Those traveling through the eastern half would have described it as "scenic rolling hills"and that would have been a fair depiction of that part of the state.

Mansfield served as the dividing line between the two. While the flat uninviting farmlands of the western half were not quite as picturesque, they did provide obvious advantages with the nearly unobstructed free-flowing back-and-forth path for the vehicles and implements. The eastern half, on the other hand, was another story. Considered at one time to be ineffectual and impractical for farming, the rolling hills were left on their own to grow tall grasses and trees that served as a haven for deer, wild turkeys, and rabbits. Then contour farming was introduced to the area. Farmers were taught to leave bands of undeveloped land between the tilled soil thus providing a protection against erosion. Surprisingly, a countryside of banded hills with rich dark colored soil is uniquely attractive, almost charming when viewed from the top of a hill.

While Mansfield served as a support for the farmers as well as the small villages in the surrounding area, it also provided jobs from its abundant industry. Nearly the entire north side of town teemed with factories and industrial shops.

At the center of town was the typical town square comprised of small retail shops and restaurants. At the very core of the square was a thinly wooded area called Central Park. With its benches and tables, and quiet serenity, it was inviting to weary shoppers and even restless travelers.

Mansfield, Ohio was more than just a town. It was at the core, the very heart of the American heartland. In 1948, there were nearly as many churches as there were bars. More money was donated to charity than was gambled in the backrooms, and going to church was the "in thing" to do.

Of course, it was a different world in 1948. Mothers let their children run through the neighborhood streets with little or no regard for molesters or muggers. Houses were left unlocked, and windows opened. Keys to the family automobile were never lost because they never left the ignition.

It was an innocent time, a time when morals were important, a high regard for elders was expected, and table manners were enforced. It was a time when the American flag was respected with an honorable salute or a simple, yet, respectful hand over the heart. Men wore stylish double-breasted suits with wing-tipped shoes and crowned with matching fedoras. Women wore printed cotton dresses, neatly starched and with a hemline fashionably set below the knees. People respected God, family, and the President and generally in that order.

It was the spring of 1948. It had been a harsh and long winter, and the farmers were eager to prepare the fields for planting. Small patches of darkened snow remained on the northern slopes and hillsides. Great icicles that hung from eaves troughs slowly disappeared under the afternoon sun. The iris and crocus bravely burst their heads through the thawed ground bringing the first signs of spring.

Twenty-one year-old Phyllis Irene Niebel finished polishing her black patent leather shoes and set them on the floor just close enough to the wood burning Round Oak stove to keep them warm and far enough away to keep them from getting scorched. It was Saturday night and was her habit to make ready a Sunday dress and her shoes for church the next day. Since she had agreed to teach Sunday school, she now had the added responsibility of preparing a lesson as well.

Everyone knew her as one of the most beautiful girls in her graduating class. She had short curly blond hair, a shapely figure, and her ashen skin accentuated her soft facial features and femininity.

As was her mother, Phyllis was a timid and shy girl uncommonly frightful of circumstances or events that left her intimidated or even slightly apprehensive. When she attended Mansfield High School, her classmates regarded her shyness as refreshingly charming, and this personality trait actually gained the attention of many boys. Despite her timidity, she enlivened many parties with her sense of humor and alluring wit. Any school function or private party usually always had Phyllis on top of the list of those to be invited.

From her early childhood, Phyllis never missed a chance to help others. She joined the First Christian Church at an early age and later as a young adult taught Sunday school. She was a member of the Eastern Stars, the 4 H Club, and the Naomi Shrine Lodge organizations. Because she was convinced that her mission in life was to help others, she joined these organizations and others just like them. When asked why such a shy girl would belong with so many organizations, she always replied that it was therapy to overcome her shyness; yet, everyone knew that it was actually because of her love for people.

Phyllis began working at the Ohio Textile Products company on October 8, 1945, shortly after graduating from high school. Her flawless record as billing clerk earned her the praise of C.S. Lake, the president of the company.

Phyllis still lived at home with her parents, John and Nolena Niebel. Her brother, Russ was 22 and was living in Chicago, while her other brother, Loyal, was 24 and living in a small town near Mansfield called Five Points.

The Niebels lived in a large, square shaped two-story house with a sun porch and a two-car garage. Although it had a Main Street address, it was located nearly three miles north of town virtually in the middle of a cornfield. The house was certainly not isolated with neighbors on either side and across the road, but it was a rural setting, rural in the sense that the neighbors' houses were far more distant than what could be found in the city. The Niebels moved there when John accepted a job at the Mansfield Reformatory as Superintendent of the reformatory farm twenty years before.

There was a gentle knock on the door, and Phyllis already knew who it was. It was her best friend Alice McKinley who lived only three doors down. Alice was a pretty girl with rich dark hair that flowed gently over her shoulders, fair skin, and a forever smile that seem to brighten the room.

It was not uncommon for her to call on Phyllis especially on a Saturday night. Even though Phyllis had a boyfriend, Alice considered it her duty to "fix her up" with someone new. It wasn't that she disapproved of her boyfriend; it was merely the excitement of the game.

Phyllis opened the front door, and an excited Alice stepped inside.

A wide-eyed Alice grabbed Phyllis by the arms. "Guess who's down at the Mansfield Diner right now as we speak," she said, her voice loud and high pitched.

Phyllis turned and walked away. Alice followed.

"Once and for all, Alice," she said taking a seat on the living room couch. "I have a boyfriend."

Alice sat down beside her. "You'll never guess."

"Well, you got that part right."

"Who was the cutest guy in our class?"

Phyllis pondered the question. "I give up."

"John Gibbs."

Phyllis turned with a surprised look. "John Gibbs! He wasn't the cutest boy in our class."

"Yes, he was, and he asked about you not ten minutes ago."

Phyllis turned and smiled. "He did?"

"Yes, he did. Now let's get in your car and go down there right now."

"I can't," said Phyllis her smile disappearing. "I have my Sunday school lesson to write yet."

"You can do it later."

She thought for a moment. "What if Raymond sees me?"

Alice leaned back. "As far as I know, you two haven't exchanged vows, have you?"

"Of course not."

"Well, then…"

"We have an understanding."

"What kind of understanding?"

"We only date one another."

Alice got to her feet. "Not binding in a court of law. Now let's go."

Phyllis paused, and then forced a smile. "I can't. It just wouldn't be right."

"You are too good to be true, Phyllis Niebel," she said putting her hands on her hips. "Well, I don't have any binding contracts or understandings, so I'm going down there." She marched over to the front door and opened it. "This is your last chance."

"Sorry."

Alice walked out of the house. "Later," she muttered without turning around.

Phyllis closed the door behind her and sauntered into the kitchen where her mother was just finishing the dishes.

Nolana Parrish Niebel was born in Licking County on November 25, 1896. She met and married John Niebel, and they had three children, Russ, Loyal, and Phyllis. Described as a "happy" person, Nolana had a smile for just about everyone she met. If someone pulled into the driveway and needed help, she was the first one on the porch.

Despite her outgoing, gregarious manner, Nolana shared a common characteristic with her daughter, Phyllis. They both were somewhat timid and shy, Phyllis more so than her mother was, and they both were frightened by just about anything loud or unusual. It was said by friends and family that the saying, "scared of her own shadow", was started because of Phyllis.

A brilliant woman with an I.Q. much higher than average, Nolana taught school before meeting and marrying John. Her remarkable intelligence coupled with her warm, amicable personality made her a favorite teacher not only with her superiors but with her students as well. She was unofficially proclaimed Teacher of the Year by more than one class that she taught.

Looking a little depressed, Phyllis took a seat at the kitchen table.

Her mother picked up a bowl and wiped it dry with a dishcloth.

"Why so glum?" asked Nolana.

"I don't know," said Phyllis.

"What did Alice want?"

"She came to tell me that John Gibbs is at the diner right now and was asking about me."

"And that has you depressed?"

"It's not just that."

"What is it then?"

"It just seems that my relationship with Raymond is going nowhere."

"Do you love him?"

Phyllis turned to her mother. She had never asked such a personal question before. "I suppose so."

Nolana hung the dishcloth on a hook over the sink and sat down at the table. "You suppose so? That doesn't sound a great endorsement of the relationship. What about Raymond? Does he love you?"

"That's just it. He says he does, but nothing ever changes," said Phyllis. "I swear I'm just a buddy of his, someone to talk to."

"Doesn't sound like there's much passion in this relationship. It sounds like you two have been married for years."

Phyllis played with the salt shaker that was in the middle of the table. "Even when he says he loves me, I don't believe it. Sounds like he's just going through the motions like reading a greeting card or something."

Nolana took a deep breath and plopped both hands on the table. "I think you should go down there and see this John Gibbs."

Phyllis stopped fidgeting with the salt shaker and looked at her mother. "You're kidding."

"I think you should shake things up a bit."

"I can't believe you're telling me this," said Phyllis.

"Well, it's not like you're married or even engaged for that matter."

"But it's a relationship just the same."

"A pretty dull one in my eyes," said her mother. "You need to add a little spice to it. See what Raymond is made of."

"It won't make any difference," said Phyllis.

"What do you mean?"

"In the first place, there's no way you could make Raymond jealous, and even if you did, he wouldn't do anything about it."

"That's too bad," said Nolana. "It's just my opinion that if a man loves you, really loves you, he will fight for you. He will do whatever it takes."

Phyllis thought for a moment. "Sorry, I just couldn't do it."

Nolana patted the back of Phyllis' hand. "You're a good girl, Phyllis. You know what's right and wrong."

"Maybe I'm too good," she said with a solemn look.

"What do you mean?"

"Oh, I don't know," she said playing with the tablecloth. "Here I am going on twenty-one and still not married."

"Is that a problem?"

"It is for me," said Phyllis. "I want a husband and kids. You know that I always have wanted that."

"It will happen. You'll see."

"Not with Raymond, it won't."

"You'll meet the right guy," she said with a confident smile. "He'll come into your life. You'll see."

Chapter Three

It was April 1, 1948. John Coulter West stepped through the doorway, and a steel gate slammed shut behind him. He took a deep breath of air and smiled as he let it go. It felt good to be free once again. He silently promised himself that he would do nothing that would risk being put back inside that place. He also knew that someday he would surely break that promise.

He scanned the parking lot until his eyes fell on a dark sedan. A man in a denim jacket got out and raised one hand. As promised, it was his old friend, Frank Thompson. With his mother sick and his father not heard from in several years, West had no one else to call.

"Thank God you made it," said West taking his friend's hand.

Frank smiled. "I'll bet you'll be glad to get away from here."

"You have no idea," said West and skirted around the front of the car. Both men got in and drove off.

"Couldn't believe you're still livin' in Parkersburg," said West.

"Why? What's wrong with that?" asked Frank.

"Not a thing. In fact, I still live there. I just figured you'd be livin' in some fancy place like New York or something like that."

"Nope. Parkersburg is my home. I can't imagine living anywhere else."

The car sped through the neighborhoods on its way to a state route that would take them back to West Virginia. It was a warm spring day, and West smiled as he gazed out the window. Women in tattered flower dresses bent over picking up last winter's debris. Small children dressed in coats and hats that were now too small marched in pairs, heads bent on their way to school. It seemed so serene, so idealistically perfect in so many ways. It didn't seem fair. People were living their lives, living the American dream and not really knowing it. Too hot. Too cold. Too much work to do. Not enough money. Living the dream and still not happy. Still not good enough. Always more and more. Why couldn't they just be happy with what they have? Why couldn't he have had a piece of the dream? A loving mother…a father who would always come home. It would be a small house with a white picket fence and sticks to be picked up. John's smile turned to a sober, glassy-eyed stare. The houses and marching school children sped by unnoticed now.

"You all right?" asked Frank, his voice shattering the silence.

"Yeah…yeah, I'm fine.

"I thought that I lost you for a minute."

West said nothing.

Frank shifted his weight and turned to West with a smile. "I don't know about you, but I could go for some eggs, meat and a pile of fluffy hash browns."

That seemed to hit a nerve with West. "Only if it comes with hot coffee as well," he said coming out of his trance.

"I wouldn't have it any other way."

Frank found a roadside diner at the outskirts of town and stopped. It was an old wooden building in need of repair. Leaning slightly to one end, it seemed to disappear into the ground. It was dark inside. Leather-skinned men dressed in bib overalls surrounded tables and talked of corn prices and weather that never seemed to cooperate. The two men found a table near a window and buried their heads in menus.

West cleared his throat and peered over the top of the menu. "Ain't going to forget what you did here today. Gonna pay you for the gas, but right now I'm a little short."

"Hey, what are friends for?" said Frank.

West stammered. "What I mean to say is I can't even pay for this meal."

"Hey, this breakfast is on me," Frank said with a smile and a big voice. "Now get whatever you want."

A gaunt woman near forty wearing a food-stained faded white uniform set two glasses of water on one end of the table. She had straw-colored hair that scattered in all directions, and a cigarette hanging from her mouth with ashes that seemed to defy gravity. She removed a half-chewed pencil from behind her ear, scratched her head with it and pressed the point on a small pad of green paper.

"What will you have?" she snarled.

Frank leaned back. "I'll have scrambled eggs, sausage patties, toast and the biggest pile of hash browns in the world."

"Coffee?"

"Yes, please."

There was a pause as she finished writing.

She glanced at West. "And what about you?"

"I'll have the same."

She jotted a quick note and disappeared into the kitchen.

West scanned the room. "Kinda dirty, isn't it?"

"Best place on earth to get a good meal," said Frank. "A clean diner means ain't nobody eatin' there."

"Suppose you're right."

They both fumbled and fidgeted.

"It must be good to get out of that prison."

"What's that?"

"Your release. Must be good to get out of there."

"Oh, yeah. Feels great."

"What was it like?" asked Frank. "You know, what's it like inside?"

"I don't want to ever go back inside that place."

"Hard life?"

"Really hard."

"Ever have any trouble with other inmates?"

"There were a lot of mean guys in there, but Daniels protected me."

"Who was Daniels?"

"A friend of mine."

"Is he still inside?"

"No, he was released months ago. In fact, I was supposed to call him when I got out."

The waitress set two cups of coffee on the table and walked away.

Frank stirred his coffee as he watched her return to the kitchen. "Not only beautiful but skilled at her craft," he muttered sarcastically.

"Huh?" asked West sipping his coffee.

"Nothing," said Frank. "So what are you going to do now that you're a free man again?"

"Not really sure," said West. "Don't have a trade and never really held a job for more than a month or so."

"So what are you gonna do?"

"I guess I'll have to try to get a job again."

"That might be tough being an ex-con and all."

"If that don't work, I might try robbing filling stations again."

Frank whipped his head around nearly running the car into the ditch. "What did you say?"

"Robert says that guys like us will never amount to anything," said West.

"Why would he say something like that?"

"My dad told me when I was just a little kid that I would end up in jail or worse."

"Good Lord," said Frank. "Your own father told you that?"

"Don't look so surprised," said West. "I think he was right."

"Don't say that," said Frank. "You're still young. You can find a job and make something of yourself."

West turned and stared out the window. "Yes sir, I think he was right."

***

Robert Daniels walked through the backdoor and set his lunch bucket on the table. It had been over seven months since he had received his parole from the Mansfield Reformatory and had already lost two jobs and was working the third. At his first job he was a forklift driver at a steel plant. It was daytime hours and good pay, but he was terminated after three unexcused absences during his first month. He was then hired as a stock boy in a five-and-dime store. He was employed for the next three months and never missed a day of work. Unfortunately, he fell into an argument with a female customer over the price of a candy bar. She went home and complained to her husband who drove to the store to confront Daniels. Confrontation led to an argument, and the argument escalated to a fistfight. Once again, Daniels was unemployed.

By that time, Daniels had become discouraged over his attempt to adapt to the working world. In all fairness, he had learned a lesson from his stay at the reformatory and had all but abandoned his life of crime. Not only had he intended to earn a respectable living by hard work, he had hoped to earn the respect of the community by settling down and even possibly buying a house. However, since his first two job experiences had proven to be unsuccessful, Daniels had doubts he could ever fit into mainstream society. It wasn't that he had a low regard or a lack of genuine respect for the blue-collar life. In fact, he sometimes drove slowly through the neighborhoods admiring the houses and lawns. He gazed, enviously, at the families having a picnic in the backyard or the father playing catch with his son in the street.

It was all too perfect, all too beautiful. It was much too perfect for Daniels. Why did it happen for all of them and not for him? The wife, kids, and the house all were a part of the American dream but not for him. It just wasn't fair. Sure he had done a few bad things in his life, but they shouldn't keep him from enjoying the good life. Chances were, if you asked Mister John Q. Public how he became apart of the American dream, he would most certainly tell you that it was nothing more, nothing less than good old fashioned hard work, and he would tell you that with an air of arrogance and impertinence. It was no wonder that Daniels had come to hate Mister John Q. Public, hate him enough to want to kill him.

Daniels' mother shuffled into the kitchen and picked up his lunch bucket.

"Did you get enough to eat?" she asked spilling the empty wrappers and a half-eaten sandwich onto the counter.

"It was a good lunch, ma," he replied taking a seat at the table.

Nearing fifty years of age and suffering from arthritis, Mrs. Robert Daniels walked slowly, her back hunched slightly. She was a proud woman, church going, and a quiet yet helpful neighbor. Her dark brown hair now seasoned with silver scattered unkempt across her head. Deep lines of worry etched her prematurely aging face exposing a sorrow that seemed to be consuming the very being of this woman.

"Are things okay at work?"

"What's that supposed to mean?"

"I was just asking," she said, rinsing his lunch bucket under the spigot.

"Sounded like criticism to me."

"No, son," she said, her voice fading with every word. "I'm just concerned, that's all. You've had some problems in the past."

Daniels was now agitated. His eyebrows were furrowed, and his lips set in a straight line. "Where's Pop?" he asked changing the subject of conversation.

"He went bowling with Bob from next door."

"Oh, in other words, he's gone out drinking," said Daniels. "That seems to be the way he forgets."

"Forgets what, Robert?" she asked. "What is it that you think your father needs to forget?"

Daniels grabbed the edge of the table with both hands and leaned forward. "It's about his life, Ma, his wretched life. He wants it to go away even if it's for a few hours."

Mrs. Daniels stood straight, her face filled with indignation and her voice defensive. "There's nothing wrong with your father's life. How dare you."

"You don't get it, do you, ma?" he said his voice growing louder. "I see it in his face. I see it in the faces of all the men who trudge off to work. All the dreams he had as a child and especially the ones he carried into adulthood are gone. He stepped over them on his way to work. Actually, he pounded them into the ground while walking to work. I never knew a man who didn't have a dream. Oh, it might be something simple like becoming the best guy on the assembly line. Others might really want to become a fireman. All kids dream about becoming a fireman, and some kids never lose that dream. Others want to become a baseball player, and some want to own their own business. They all have dreams and when that dream dies in that man's heart, a big piece of him dies too."

Mrs. Daniels pulled a hankie from her dress pocket and dried her eyes. "Don't tell me anymore," she sobbed.

"Remember when Pop had that certain spark in his eyes. Some people call it a twinkle. When he comes, home from work today, take a look at his eyes. In fact, look deep into his eyes and see if you see that spark. It's gone. It died with his plans and dreams. It died when he married you."

Mrs. Daniels turned with a look of wrath. "Don't you dare blame me for this? We got married, had you, and he went to work to support us."

"It's not a question of blame. What Pop did is what every man does. It's expected of him. He gets married, raises a family, works for forty odd years, and waits to die. But the sad part is the day when he finally realizes his dreams are never going to happen. That's the day when that light goes out in his eyes. That's the day when he discovers that booze makes him forget."

Mrs. Daniels wiped her eyes and took a deep breath. "Please stop. I love your dad, and what you're saying hurts."

"Sure it hurts, ma. Sure it hurts, but what about Pop? How much is he hurting?"

She said nothing.

"It might be enough for Pop, but it's not enough for me. I want more. I want more than just an eight-to-five, kids and a house. I want it all, and I don't want to pay the price to get it."

Her face went blank as she turned once again to her son. "What do you mean by that?"

"I'm not working for pennies and spending dollars. I'm not saving my nickels and dimes to buy something when I can take it away from someone else."

"Oh, please don't say that," she said her face wrought with sorrow. "Your father and I want nothing but the best for you. If you go back to your old ways, you'll end up back there in that prison."

Daniels got to his feet. "The only thing I can promise you is I'll never go back to that place." He stared at her for a moment, turned and walked out of the room.

The following days drifted into weeks. Daniels made a genuine effort to conform to mainstream society. With few exceptions, he generally came straight home after work and spent evenings either with his parents or reading a book in his room. As a favor to his mother, he even attended church services with them one Sunday. That turned out to be a one-time experience, since Daniels declared that he didn't need any of that "God stuff", as he put it.

Despite that, his parents were proud of his effort. Daniels was going to work everyday and had even taken on some of the duties and chores around the house. For the most part, Daniels was content with his life. He knew that this was the right thing to do, but there was something that would not stop nagging at him. Something deep inside him was pulling at him...pulling him down a road of crime and evil.

He tried to ignore it, but it all seemed to come unraveled one warm night in May of 1948. Mr. Daniels had been drinking and was sitting on the front porch swing. He was a big man with broad shoulders and massive arms that were adorned with an array of tattoos. He had a wide nose that appeared to have been broken at one time or another, and it seemed as if he never was without a cigarette hanging from his lips. He had a mild manner about him, quiet by nature. He was slow to anger but a force to avoid when he was riled.

It was nearly midnight. It had been unseasonably warm that day, and, despite the late hour, the night air had still not chilled. A car pulled into the driveway and came to an abrupt stop about halfway. The driver's side door opened, and Daniels spilled out of the car and sprawled out onto the lawn. Empty bottles followed rolling down the driveway and into the street.

He managed to get to his feet and stumbled his way towards the front of the house. He stopped at the front porch and gulped from the bottle in his hand. Almost as a return salute, his father sipped from his.

"Hey there, old man," he said staggering in place.

Mr. Daniels said nothing.

"Oh, that's right. You're a quiet drinker, not like your son who gets a bit mouthy as some would say. I like to think of myself as a bit verbose. What do you think, Pop? Am I a fallen down, loud mouth, pain in the ass drunk, or am I merely a little boisterous? Surely you have an opinion in this matter."

Mr. Daniels leaned back in the porch swing but said nothing.

"Still ain't talkin', huh, Pop?" He staggered to the first step, turned, and sat on the edge of the porch. "Can't say as I blame you. Your darlin' son didn't turn out quite the way you planned.

Gotta believe a son like me would make the Pope turn into an alcoholic."

Daniels turned and looked at his father. He had no expression. He just stared blankly straight ahead.

"Here we are, the two of us like strangers sitting on a train," said Daniels turning back to face the street. "Both going someplace and not really knowing where. Oh, I know, it's all my fault. Here I am, twenty-four years old, fresh out of prison and living back home. What a disappointment I must be. Must be embarrassing when the neighbor asks, 'How's that boy of yours doing?' Must make you cringe. Tell me Pop. Do you lie and tell them I'm some big executive with a major corporation, or do you tell them the truth that your son is a loser and always will be? The worst part is and always will be how I failed you. You had such big plans for me. I was the apple of your eye, as they say. You always thought I'd be some big shot seeing as how I had such good grades. I guess if I had gone to college like you wanted me to, I might be that big shot by now. I wanted to be a big league baseball player. Not sure if I was good enough...I always thought so."

Daniels drained the bottle and tossed it into the yard.

"Can't tell you why I do the things I do. Never thought when I was a kid I'd be doing shit like this. Don't remember ever stealin' anything. Oh, maybe a candy bar or some such stuff. Nothing big though. I even remember how indignant I would get over bank robbers. The nerve of them guys. Get a job, I'd say. Now, here I am, no better than them."

Daniels paused for a moment hoping for a response.

"Bet you're wondering where I went wrong. Well, I gotta tell ya, it set me to wondering as well. I know it sounds like a cop out, but there's a voice deep inside me that keeps nagging me. It tells me I have a right to all the stuff other people have, and it tells me to take it from them. I know how that must sound, but it's the truth. It never leaves me alone. It constantly nags at me until I can't stand it anymore. Sometimes, I think I'm going crazy. Maybe, I'm just evil, born to be bad."

He flopped down onto the porch and closed his eyes. "No question about it," he muttered. "I'm just plain evil." A moment later, he was snoring.

Mr. Daniels slowly gathered up his empty bottles and got to his feet. He started for the door and paused over his son. "I love you, boy," he muttered aloud. "Always have and always will."

Chapter Four

The hot days of summer came early that year. It was the first week of June and already the temperatures were soaring into the nineties. Windows and doors remained open for relief from the heat; screen doors hooked for security. Despite the discomfort, farmers were excited about the bumper crops promised by the early spring rains and the unseasonably hot days.

It was late morning, and already the temperature was in the eighties. Dark clouds threatened rain and brought a moisture-laden air that seemed to saturate everything and everybody in its path.

Nolena Niebel opened her door to, yet, another guest. They politely exchanged greetings and pleasantries, and the neatly dressed lady took a seat with the others.

For years the farmer's wives in the area met once a week at various members' homes. Since it was centrally located and had ample room for accommodating such a large gathering, the Niebel home was chosen more often than any of the others.

They called themselves the Willing Club. They made clothing, quilts, and canned harvested produce all for the charitable and noble cause of donating them to families in need. Not only was the club begun for its benevolent goals, it also served as a get-together for the women to catch up on the latest news and gossip.

There was a knock on the door, and Nolena opened it. It was Mrs. Cox who lived a few doors down the street. She took her place next to one of the others and announced that Velma Statler wouldn't be attending today. She was feeling a bit ill and had taken to her bed. Eyes rolled as Mrs. Cox made her announcement. It wasn't the first time that Velma Statler had missed a meeting because of her alleged illnesses. Lately, it had been happening on a regular basis. It was rumored without contention that her illness was self-induced. With a wink of the eye and the motion of the arm as if taking a drink, one woman would silently communicate with another.

"Come on, ladies. Who are we kidding?" said Susan Harlan, leaning back in her chair. "Velma has a drinking problem. We all know it. We just don't talk about it."

"She has a right, you know," said Catherine Watson. "Losing her son in the war like that."

"There were a lot of people who lost someone in the war and didn't become an alcoholic," said Mrs. Cox.

"All I know is that I smelled something on her breath last week when we met," said Sharon Dobbs.

Everyone exchanged glances. Nobody was quite sure how far to take this topic of conversation. It was fun and self-serving to talk about Velma behind her back, but everyone knew that if they pursued this discussion any further it would most certainly be considered gossip by anybody's definition.

"Well, ladies," said Nolena, with an uplifted voice meant to change the subject. "What will we do today? We finished that bedspread last week.

Mrs. Cox picked up a magazine and waved it in her face. "It's too hot. I say we do nothing."

"We can't just do nothing," said Catherine. "The whole point is to make something to give to others."

"It must be ninety degrees in here," said Sharon.

"I just want to talk," said Susan. "Especially, about the drunken Velma."

Mrs. Cox laughed aloud. "Aren't you terrible?"

Nolena closed her eyes and shook her head. "There should be some kind of rule that says you can't talk about one of the members when they're not here to defend themselves."

"What could she possibly say in her own defense?" said Susan, more as a statement than a question.

"In all fairness, ladies," said Nolena, "Whoever heard of even a drunkard indulging this early in the day?"

Sharon sat up and stuck a finger in the air. "Last week, I saw Ida Benson coming out of a bar on Third Street, and it couldn't have been one o'clock in the afternoon."

There was a pause while everyone tried to remember who Ida Benson was. They all sat back in their chairs and fanned themselves.

"God, it's hot," said Mrs. Cox.

"Suppose to hit ninety," said Sharon, wiping her forehead with a hankie.

Catherine cleared her throat and shifted in her chair. "Frank said he heard that one inmate tried to escape the other day."

"Is that a fact?" Sharon asked.

Catherine turned to Nolena. "Did John say anything about it?"

"Not a thing. Of course, John is outside all the time and doesn't hear much about what's going on."

"You'd think the news of something like that would travel all through that place," said Catherine."

Nolena tilted her head high as if to say she had been offended. "John doesn't talk much about his work or anything about that God forsaken place for that matter."

"Has anybody ever escaped from there?" asked Catherine."

"Not that I ever heard of," said Mrs. Cox.

"Seems strange," said Catherine. "You'd think that someone would have made it out of there by now."

Catherine tightened her face and shuddered. "That has always scared me. You know the first thing that they will do is break into one of the homes around here."

"What do you suppose they would do then?" asked Sharon.

"Well, you know what I'm talking about. They would take advantage of you," said Catherine. "Lord knows they are animals and wouldn't hesitate for a moment."

"You're getting yourself all worked up for nothing," said Sharon.

"Don't kid yourself. They're all criminals. That's why they're locked up in that place."

"Just because they robbed a grocery store doesn't mean they will have their way with you," said Sharon.

"Doesn't mean they won't either."

"Okay, girls," said Nolena. "We're getting a little carried away here. Let's, at least, decide what we'll work on next month."

"How 'bout a chastity belt for Catherine so she won't get raped," said Sharon.

Catherine snarled.

"I think we should start another quilt," said Susan Harlan.

"In ninety degree heat?" asked Mrs. Cox.

"If we start now, we'll have it finished by winter," said Susan.

"She's right," said Nolena. "The last one we started in the winter and finished it in July."

"Sounds good to me," said Sharon.

"Then it's settled," said Nolena.

Chapter Five

An older Pontiac stopped in front of a small, four-room house. Low hanging branches from silver maples partially hid the Cape Cod from view. Plywood resting on two posts covered the front doorway, while a dirty, brown-haired dog roamed the front yard, his boundaries set by a rope around his neck.

John West said his good byes to his friend, Frank, grabbed his suitcase from the back seat, and started for the front door. Even though he hadn't seen his mother in a very long time, he was still reluctant to step inside. His father left years ago, and it seemed as if his mother was sick with one thing or another ever since he left. She was not a strong woman and was prone to sickness. West had always wondered how many times was she actually sick and how many times it was hypochondria.

West opened the front door and stepped inside. She wasn't lying on the sofa, which surprised him. He couldn't remember a time she wasn't on the sofa with an illness or an ache of some kind. He stepped into the kitchen, and there she was sitting at the table head in hands. She was a sad looking woman aged beyond her years. Her flowered dress was faded and torn, her hair unkempt and streaked with gray. It was if her life had become a series of depressing, unfortunate incidences, and she was living in this self-inflicted abyss of sorrow.

"Ma," said West with a soft voice.

She quickly tilted her head. "John," she said with a startled voice. She wiped her face with a hankie. "How are you, son?"

"I'm fine, ma. How are you?"

"Oh, I don't know. Been fighting the flu lately. I got your letter. That's great that you are getting out early. What does it mean when they say you're on parole?"

"It just means I have to behave myself, follow some rules and report to a parole officer."

She ran her hands through her hair in a futile attempt to comb it. "I knew you'd be a good boy in there, and that they would let you go."

West set his suitcase on the floor and took a seat across the table from his mother. "So how are you getting along?"

"Oh, I'm getting by. Thank God, the house was paid for when your father left. Been tough enough keeping the electric turned on."

"Heard from Pop?"

"Not a word. Someone said he's livin' with some woman half his age. Reckon he don't have time for me anymore."

West winced at the news. He glanced around the room. "Well, everything looks about the same as when I left."

"Any chance you could take a look at the roof on the outhouse?" she asked. "Started leakin' the other day. Can't imagine what would cause that."

"Sure, Ma," he said covering her outstretched hand with his. "Don't worry about a thing. I'm home."

She turned to him with a look on her face he had never seen before. "Johnnie, I need to ask you a question."

"What is it, ma?"

"Where are you planning to stay?"

West withdrew his hand and sat straight. "Well, here, of course."

"I'm sorry, but I can't let you."

"What are you talking about?"

"I can't let you stay here," she said with a tear falling down her face. She reached into her pocket and pulled out a twenty-dollar bill. "Here, take this and get yourself a room downtown."

West took the money and stared at his mother. "Why can't I stay here?"

She took a deep breath and let it out. "I have a boyfriend, and he doesn't want you here."

"I won't be a bother. I'll sleep on the couch."

"You can't stay."

"Why, Mother? I got a right to know."

She glanced down at the age spots that dappled the backs of her hands. "He don't like convicts and won't live in the same house with one."

"But Ma, this is my house too. I grew up here."

"I know, son, but I just can't take a chance."

"Take a chance? Ma, this is your son talking. We're blood. You'd kick me out over this guy?"

She reached across the table and firmly took his hands. "Johnnie, look at me. I'm an old woman. I got more problems than you can imagine. I'm so sick half the time I can't walk to the store for a quart of milk. Most of the time, I can't even afford that quart of milk, and along comes a man who likes me and can help me with my bills."

"But, Ma..."

She squeezed his hands. "Johnnie, this is probably my last chance. I don't want to end up alone. I'm begging you to please do this for me."

West said nothing.

"Please Johnnie. I don't want to live my life alone."

He slowly got to his feet and stuffed the money in his pocket. "Alright, Ma, but he'd better be good to you."

"Thanks, Johnnie," she said forcing a smile. She got to her feet, opened a cupboard door and grabbed a letter that was stuck between two drinking glasses. "In the beginning, I kept all your mail. After a while, it pretty much stopped coming, and I realized that what I had saved was just ads and stuff. Wouldn't be much good to you, so I threw 'em out." She handed him the letter. "This came for you just last week. I had just got your letter about getting out, so I saved this one. It's from Columbus, Ohio. Some guy by the name of Daniels."

Johnnie studied the return address and smiled.

Chapter Six

John Elmer Niebel got out of his car and started for the side door of his house. He was a stocky man just six feet tall with broad shoulders and narrow hips. He was a handsome man with a square jaw, fair skin, and a firm but kind face. He seldom smiled and for that was regarded by many as a mean person. In reality, he was a stern, uncompromising man who believed in strict discipline, obedience to rules and laws and had a high regard for living a Christian life. The only time that he was ever actually mean was when he confronted someone who disagreed with his high standards and principles.

John was born in 1898 in a small town in the farmlands of Ohio called Mt. Vernon. As an adult and family man, he held many different jobs until he accepted the position of superintendent of the farm system of the Mansfield Reformatory. Essentially, he managed the operation of the gardens, the hog and cattle farms, and the farming of the field corn and soybeans. Actually, it was a vibrant and very lucrative business. Nearly all the meat was butchered at the prison and was used to supply Mansfield Reformatory and the other prisons in Ohio. The gardens produced a harvest of vegetables that were canned at the prison and helped feed Ohio prisoners as well.

He was well paid, but it was a very stressful and demanding job. With no assistant, he was on call 24 hours a day for any problem that would arise, and with his high regard for job responsibility, he would never shirk or avoid a problem regardless of the time of day. He always said how grateful he was that he had married such an understanding woman.

John walked through the side door and into the kitchen. Sausage patties and thinly sliced potatoes crackled on the stove filling the kitchen with mouth-watering smells.

"Something smells good," he said with a smile.

Nolana was setting the table. "Sausage and fried potatoes," she said without looking up.

John lightly kissed her on the cheek and glanced at the table. "Only two plates?"

"Phyllis is on a date."

"All the more fried potatoes for me."

"Go wash up," she said scooping the food into bowls. "It's ready."

John washed his hands and splashed water in his face. It had been a hot day, and the water felt good on his tired face. It was his custom to wear his suit coat at the table, but the temperature had soared to over ninety degrees, so he removed his coat and hung it on the back of a chair.

"Looks good," he said taking a seat at the table.

"Thought you deserved one of your favorites," she said taking a seat across the table.

"Why? What did I do to deserve such a meal?" he said sticking a forkful of potatoes in his mouth.

"It's not what you did but rather what you're going to do," she said her smile disappearing.

John froze. "And what's that?"

"You're going to take me on a vacation."

"Vacation? What are you talking about?"

"I want to go on a vacation. Simple as that."

"What brought this on?"

"I'm just tired and need to get away."

John scooted his chair from the table. "Nolana, I can't just up and take off."

Nolana became excited, her eyes aglow. "We don't have to go right away. It's early in the summer. We could plan one for later."

"Oh, I don't know," he said wiping his mouth with his napkin. "It's not that easy to get away. It's the middle of the growing season, harvest is coming up."

"John, we've only been on three vacations in our married lives. It's time for number four," she said with a stern voice.

John paused. "Where would we go?"

"Who cares? As long as it's away from here, I don't care where it is."

"Well, we can't afford to go too far."

Nolana leaned forward. "Niagara Falls. You promised to take me there for our honeymoon, and you never did."

John thought for a moment and glanced at his plate. The food was getting cold, and he wondered if he would ever get to finish his meal.

"Oh, okay," he said returning to his supper. "Go ahead and make plans. I'll make arrangements to get some time off. Now, can I eat my meal?"

"Thanks, John," she said with a smile. "You won't regret it. We'll keep it simple. In fact, I'll bring food along to make our meals. That will save a little money."

"Okay, okay. Now, let's eat."

Silence fell on the room as they finished their dinner. John could tell that she wanted to tell him more. Probably gossip she had heard or something about the kids that he should know. He began to feel sorry for her and regret his being short with her.

"Anything happen today?" he asked wiping his plate with a slice of bread.

"Oh, not much. Didn't get much housecleaning done today," she said wiping her forehead. "Just too darn hot."

"It was a hot one today. That's for sure."

"Mrs. Cox said that she saw Velma Crider coming out of a bar in the early afternoon the other day."

John looked up. "That doesn't necessarily prove anything."

"Well, she's missed more than one of our club meetings because of some illness, and there have been other times when alcohol has been smelled on her breath.

"Even though I don't approve of drinking alcohol, what she does in her own home doesn't concern me."

"Oh, you're so right," she said with a playful tone and inflection in her voice.

"I think the only reason that you women get together is to gossip. That's what I think."

"That's a cruel thing to say, Mr. Niebel," she said. "I think our club serves a very useful purpose by helping others."

John smiled but said nothing. He pushed back from the table, unfolded the newspaper and snapped it to life.

Chapter Seven

It was July 4, 1948. An older model car stopped in front of the Pink Flamingo Motel in Columbus. The building was in total disrepair with weeds growing through the cracks in the pavement and peeled paint lying in piles that marked a path around the walls. John West turned off the engine and got out of the car. It was nearly noon, and, for the most part, he had explicitly followed the instructions in Robert Daniels' letter. He was to stand in front of the Pink Flamingo Motel at twelve o'clock on the Fourth of July. West was fifteen minutes early, and, other than that, he had done everything that Daniels had asked.

It was after one in the afternoon when one of the doors opened. Daniels emerged wearing only his shorts. He squinted into the afternoon sun trying to recognize the figure leaning against a car, arms folded and staring at him.

"Is that you, Johnnie?" asked Daniels with a cautious smile.

West started across the parking lot. "Man, am I ever glad to see you," he said sticking out his hand.

"You old bastard," said Daniels taking his hand. "How ya doing?"

"Doin' great."

Daniels opened the door. "Here, come on inside."

It was a small room with two single beds. There were no blankets, and the sheets had turned gray. There were stains on the carpet, and a faded picture of a bowl of fruit was hanging on the wall.

They stepped inside, and Daniels closed the door. West glanced around the room. There was only one chair, and it was full of dirty clothes.

Daniels pointed at one of the beds. "Have a seat."

West slowly eased himself onto the edge of the bed, while Daniels pushed the clothes off the chair and sat down.

"So, how do you like being a free man again?" asked Daniels.

"Feels great," he said. "Just can't seem to find a job."

"I thought you were living at home with your mother."

"I did until she kicked my ass out."

"Why'd she do that?"

"Her boyfriend doesn't like convicts."

A stern, determined look came over Daniels face. "Wanna go kick his ass?"

West pushed on the bed to check the springs. "Nah, that's alright. I got no business living with my mother anyhow."

"That's exactly what I did," said Daniels. "After I lost my third job, they both wouldn't let me hear the end of it."

"Sorry, man, but I didn't bring much money with me," said West. "I'm down to my last five dollars. Maybe I can find a job in this town."

"Forget it," said Daniels. "We're through with all that."

"Huh?"

Some people are just not cut out for the nine-to-five life."

"We still need money," said West.

"Oh, I agree," said Daniels, with a wiry smile. "I just ain't gonna punch a time clock to get it."

"You mean…"

"I mean we're going to take from the rich and give to us, the poor."

West frowned and looked away.

"Don't you get it? We're going to rob a few gas stations. That's all."

"I just don't want to go back to that prison," said West.

"We ain't going back to that place, my friend," said Daniels. "That you can count on."

West paused for a moment then shrugged his shoulders. "I'm in," he said aloud. "What the hell do I have to lose?"

Daniels smiled at his small victory of gaining a partner. "Do you have a gun?"

West pulled back his suit coat. A small, pearl handle jutted over his belt. He said nothing but smiled proudly of his prize possession.

"How's your car working?"

"Fine. Why?"

"We don't need two cars, so tomorrow I'm going to sell mine and buy me a gun."

West leaned back and sprawled across the bed. "I need a nap," he said.

"Not a bad idea," said Daniels. "We're going to need plenty of rest today, because tomorrow we're going to be busy."

It was nearly noon the next day when they finally got out of bed. Both men woke with empty stomachs, but with only a few dollars between them, they decided to keep what they had. Instead, Daniels would take West to a place where they could eat all they wanted for free. West was dubious but just curious enough to investigate. They both got in the car, and Daniels turned down one street and then another. Soon they were driving slowly down a deserted alley. Daniels scanned one side and then the other until he pointed at the back of a building and told West to stop. It was the rear of a diner with six trash cans, three on either side of the back door.

"There's lunch," said Daniels with an excited voice.

West studied the alley then turned to Daniels. "What are you talking about?"

"We're too late for breakfast, said Daniels with a smile. "The eggs and bacon are cold and buried under lunch leftovers."

West followed Daniels' line of sight. He hoped that he was wrong, so he followed it again.

"You're not talking about those trash cans, are you?" asked West.

"You'd be surprised what rich people don't eat."

"You mean to tell me you want me to open one of those trash cans and eat the food?"

"Some of it is still warm."

"That's garbage," said West his mouth agape.

Daniels pointed at one of the cans. "I guarantee there is a New York Strip steak in one of those cans. It may not be as big as when it started, but if it was served to a woman, you can bet we're getting a bigger piece than what she ate. For some reason, women don't clean off their plates. Hell, they eat a salad and then pick at the dinner."

West stared at Daniels for a moment, turned to the trash cans, and then back to Daniels. "So what's next?"

"We wait."

"Wait for what?"

"Wait for a guy in a sloppy white uniform to dump a load in the cans. That way, we're getting the freshest food, and we don't have to worry about him opening the door while we're diving for food."

The two men sat quietly for a few minutes staring at the backdoor. As predicted, the door opened, and a man emptied a metal can into one of the trash cans.

"Someone just rang the dinner bell," said Daniels with a triumphant smile. He walked over to the can, removed the lid and handed it to West. He carefully rooted through the garbage until he found two partly eaten hamburgers for West and he settled for the remains of a very large pork chop. They took the food and returned to the car.

West stared at the two pieces of meat lying in his lap. One had a small, half-moon bite taken from it while the other was nearly half gone. "I can't believe I'm eating garbage. We should have at least found the bun to go with it."

"You can't think of it as garbage," said Daniels taking a bite from his pork chop. Imagine that we just went to one of those drive-in restaurants, and we're eating it in the car."

West stared at the meat as if it were tainted. "But they have bites taken from them. I can see where the teeth bit them."

Daniels smiled. "Imagine that it was some gorgeous woman who bit into them. Chances are, it was. After all, how many men do you know who would waste a good hamburger?"

"With my luck, she probably rides a broom," said West, still staring at the food.

Daniels started the car and drove slowly down the alley. "Just eat the food," he said with a note of indignation.

West picked up one of the hamburgers with two fingers. He took a small bite from the uneaten side. "Hey, not bad," he said with a smile.

It was later in the day when Daniels made a call to a distant cousin who lived on the other side of town. He agreed to buy Daniels' vehicle even though it was doubtful that the car was worth what he was asking. It was assumed that it was a favor generously performed from one family member to another.

Next, Daniels looked up an old friend who had spent an incredible amount of his life in and out of jails and prisons. To no one's surprise, he had an extraordinary passion for handguns, and Daniels was able to buy from him a .25 caliber pistol. It cost him considerably less than what he had planned, so, to the delight of John West, they ate their dinner sitting at a table in an upscale restaurant near the center of town. They both had steak and French fries with pie and ice cream for dessert.

It was nearly eight o'clock when West finished his dinner and pushed back from the table. He slowly patted his stomach and wore a smile of contentment.

"That's the best meal I've had in years," he said.

Daniels leaned forward. "If we want to eat like that again, we're going to have to get some money."

The smile disappeared from West's face. "I…I suppose you're right."

"What's the matter with you?"

"I'm nervous."

"Nervous about what?"

"Robbing somebody."

"Why would that make you nervous?"

"What if they have a gun?"

"We shoot 'em," said Daniels with an evil grin. "Plain and simple."

West paused as he thought about what Daniels had said. "This is what I'm nervous about. We're headed right back to the joint."

"I told you once before," said Daniels. "I ain't going back there. I'll die first."

"That's one thing we agree on," said West. "I believe I'd rather die than go back there."

Daniels grabbed the check and got to his feet. "Let's get out of here."

It was nearly eleven o'clock when West and Daniels parked in front of a small gas station in a low-income neighborhood on the south side of town. "Fred's Gas" was handwritten on a sign that hung, precariously, from one nail. They could see an older man presumed to be Fred as he went about the business of closing for the day. He had just finished his daily reconciliation report, and was about to turn off the compressors in the shop as well as other non-essential equipment, when he noticed that two men had entered the front door. He finished his rounds by locking the back door and then walked slowly to the front.

"If you boys need gas, you're outta luck," he said wiping his hand with a rag.

Daniels pulled his gun from his coat pocket and pointed it at the man. "This is a stick up."

Fred glanced at the gun. He stopped wiping his hands for only a moment and then started again. "What the hell you all a doin'?" he asked with a smile.

West pulled out his gun. It shook so much that he pointed it at the floor for fear of it going off accidentally. "You heard what he said."

Fred smiled as he walked over to the cash register, punched a key and opened the cash drawer. He glanced at it and turned to the others.

"You boys are outta luck," he said. "There's about ten bucks in change. Are you going to risk jail for ten dollars?"

"Where's the rest of it?" asked Daniels.

"Where's the rest of what?"

"You've been open all day. You had to have taken in more than that."

"The wife stopped by a while back and took a deposit to the bank. Like I said, you guys are just plain outta luck."

"Come on," said West. "Let's get out of here."

Daniels walked over and rifled the cash drawer. "It might not be much, but we ain't leaving here empty-handed." He pocketed the money then motioned for Fred to go back into the shop. They found a piece of rope and tied him to the bumper of a car.

"I think we ought to beat the shit out of him," said West staring blankly at Fred.

"What?" said Daniels with a look of surprise.

"He's been an asshole the whole time. Hell, he's been laughing at both of us."

Daniels looked at West's hand that was holding the gun. It wasn't shaking anymore. "What the hell got into you? For a while there I thought you were gonna puke or somethin' and now you're mister tough guy."

"Look at him," said West pointing at Fred. "He's practically laughing at us." West pulled a blackjack from his pocket and started for the man.

Daniels grabbed him by the arm and pulled him towards the door. "Come on. Let's get out of here."

The next day was July 6th and it dawned hot and humid with no relief in sight. The summer had been a real "scorcher" as the newspapers described it with 59 deaths across the nation resulting from the record setting heat. During July, the temperature climbed into the nineties nearly everyday, and many days it topped the hundred-degree mark. Every store had sold out of fans, as it had become necessary to have one in nearly every room of the house.

By late afternoon, the room at the Pink Flamingo where West and Daniels were staying had reached an unbearable heat. The only fan in the room made a clanking noise and blew in only one direction. They had placed it on the windowsill hoping to suck in the cool night air, but as night turned to day and the sun rose high in the sky with no cloud protection, the tiny fan did little or no good.

John West arose and sat on the edge of the bed. It had been a restless night trying to sleep in the heat. It seemed like he had tossed and turned the whole night. He reached for a corner of the sheet and wiped his face. West looked over at Daniels asleep in the bed next to his. It wasn't fair. The heat had no affect on his sleep at all. Except for an occasional snorting sound, you would swear he had passed away during the night.

West's thoughts turned to the previous night. The very first time they did a job together, and he had failed. He knew that Daniels had seen his hand shaking. It was so obvious. His gun quivered like a leaf on a tree. Besides that, he was completely ineffectual. He had to point the gun at the floor because he had no control of it. For some reason, he couldn't look the man in the face. He was tongue-tied. Daniels had to do all the talking. In fact, if it hadn't been for Daniels, he might have been overpowered by the man. He was much bigger and stronger than West. He, obviously, had to have recognized and believed that West was a coward. He certainly showed all the signs of a coward. Yet, something happened to West. Suddenly his hand wasn't shaking, and he was aggressively more in control. He had, in fact, pulled out his blackjack and would have hit the man if Daniels hadn't stopped him. Yeah, that's right. Daniels had to hold him back. He had forgotten about that. It had been a long time since he had done a job. Obviously, he was just a little jittery. It was stage fright. That's all. Hell, he had served a stretch in the pen for robbery. Why wouldn't he be nervous? Any normal person would have been nervous. You don't spend time in jail for a crime and not think about it when you commit the crime again. Whatever the problem was, West was confident that he was over it and would hold up his end on the next job.

In the bed next to him, Daniels rolled over, his eyes open and fixed on West. Sweat beaded on his forehead; his pillow stained from the long hot night.

"What time is it?" asked Daniels.

West glanced at the alarm clock on a table between the two beds. "Almost four o'clock."

"In the afternoon?"

West, sarcastically, glanced around the room. Bright, hazy light streamed through the blinds giving the room an off-color, almost yellowish tinted light.

"Yeah, it's four in the afternoon."

Daniels got up and sat on the edge of the bed across from West. He wiped his face with the tee shirt that he was wearing. "What are you doing? You look weird sitting there staring at the floor."

"Thinking about last night."

Daniels reached for a pack of cigarettes on the nightstand. He bumped one from the pack and lit it up. "A measly ten bucks. That guy said it best when he said you guys are outta luck."

"I was thinking about how lousy I was."

"What are you talking about? You did fine."

"I was so nervous I thought I was going to puke."

"Hey, you got over it. For a while there I thought you was going to kill the man."

West's jaw tightened, his eyes became slits. "That guy was laughing at us. There we are with guns pointed at him, and he has the nerve to laugh at us."

"I don't know that you could actually say he was laughing."

West was not listening to Daniels. He was still staring at the floor. His voice by now was bold, almost thunderous. "He might laugh at me on the streets, but not when I'm holding a gun on him. He might think of me as a piece of shit, but when my thirty-eight is pointed at his head and my finger is on the trigger, he'd better, by God, give me some respect."

There was a pause. Daniels didn't know what to say. He wasn't even certain that West had finished speaking.

Daniels smiled and slapped West on the knee. "Hey, old buddy," he said, his voice upbeat. "Let's go get something to eat. It's too late for breakfast, but I know a bar near here that serves the best burger in town."

West didn't move. He was still staring at the floor between the beds. "All my life, there have been guys like him, laughing at me. I know what they're thinking. They think because I'm short and ugly, they can push me around. Because I'm not so smart, they can make fun of me. They think I won't know what they're saying since I'm retarded. Guys like that make me sick." He reached for his gun on the nightstand. He held it in his hands, caressing it as if it were a friend. "It's funny how some guys get it all, good looks, tall, plenty of money. And then there are guys like me. It just ain't fair, I tell ya. It just ain't fair."

Daniels snubbed out his cigarette and got to his feet. "Come on, my friend. Let me buy you a big, juicy hamburger with all the fixings. That'll make you feel better."

They called it Joe's Grill and Bar. While everyone else called their establishment a Bar and Grill, Joe, when he opened it in 1941, wanted to emphasize the grill rather than the bar by putting it first in the name. It was his idea that people would consider his place more as a restaurant rather than a bar. He had hoped by doing so, he would attract a broader range and possibly higher class of clientele.

Despite his limited menu, which included hamburgers, hot dogs, French fries, and baked beans, his hamburgers were legendary and attracted patrons from miles around. The secret to his success was found at a cattle ranch just outside town. The cattle were slaughtered, ground into hamburger, and delivered daily to Joe's back door. Joe, personally, shaped the ground meat into patties that were give-or-take within an ounce of a half-pound that produced the biggest and juiciest hamburger sandwiches anyone had ever eaten.

In a darkened corner booth near the rear of the bar, Robert Daniels and John West gulped down their third glass of beer while they waited for their hamburgers.

Daniels briskly rubbed his hands together in excited anticipation. "I'm telling you, you won't believe how good these burgers are."

West tipped his empty glass of beer allowing the foamy suds to drain into his mouth. "I just wish they'd hurry it up. I'm starving here," he said setting the glass on the table.

Daniels leaned forward, his voice muted. "We need to do another job tonight. We just have enough money for this meal."

West scanned the bar. "We ought to just hit this place on the way out. Looks like they might have money."

"Are you kidding?" said Daniels. "Take money from Joe's? We'd never be able to come back."

A tall, skinny woman in a grease-stained uniform set two plates of food and two more beers on the table. With nonchalance and without saying a word, she turned and walked away.

"Hope the food is better than the service," said West. He picked up a bottle of ketchup and unscrewed the top.

"What are you doing?" asked Daniels, his voice excited and somewhat demanding.

West froze. "I'm putting ketchup on my burger," he said with a surprised look.

"Oh, no, you don't," said Daniels taking the bottle from his hands. "First, try it without ketchup. You gotta taste the burger. Then, if you don't like it, you can drown it in condiments."

West picked up the burger and took a bite. Daniels sat quietly as he watched him eat.

"Damn, this is a good burger," said West.

"I told you so, my friend. Best burger in town."

West grabbed the ketchup bottle. "It still needs ketchup."

Daniels' smile disappeared. "Good God," he muttered.

"What were you saying about our needing money?" asked West, his voice garbled from a mouthful of food.

"We'll do another filling station. This time we'll stake the place out. If we see his wife coming in to take a deposit to the bank, we'll hit them then while she's got the money."

West set down his sandwich and sipped his beer. "Sounds like a good plan to me."

Daniels leaned back and looked around the bar. For as hot as it was, it was surprisingly cool in the place. Near the ceiling, a giant fan served as an exhaust pulling hot air from the room. Ceiling fans were placed over each table and booth, and the few windows were darkened with pulled blinds.

"Did ya ever dream you're a big shot executive of some sorts?" asked Daniels, staring at the slow turning exhaust fan near the ceiling.

West looked up. He said nothing.

A smile appeared on Daniel's face; his eyes glossed over in his nearly drunken state. "Wouldn't that be something? Fancy clothes, big house, and new cars in the driveway. Wouldn't that be something?"

West stopped eating. He had seen Daniels in a drunken state before, but this was different. He looked and sounded as if he were in a trance, almost as if his soul had left this earth.

"Know what I'd do if I had lots of money?" asked Daniels without waiting for or even expecting an answer. "I'd give it all to poor people, the bums, the tramps, the war-injured guys who can't get a job. There are so many guys out there who can't get a job, and it's the fat cats that sit in their ivory towers whom are to blame. Yeah, that's what I'd do. I'd make 'em rich. Make 'em so rich they could walk right into their offices and tell them to go to hell."

West smiled. "You could give me some of that money," he said, sipping his beer. "I'm one of them poor guys."

Daniels never heard a word West said. He was still in his trance-like state. "I'd go to all the fancy restaurants in town. I'd never eat at home. No, sir. No baloney sandwiches for me. Only the prettiest girls would go with me, and it damn sure would be a different one every night. No settling down for me. Love 'em and leave 'em. That's what I always say. I'd have the biggest and best cars, one for every night of the week. I probably should have some guy to drive me around all the time. You know what I mean? He would drop me off at the front door and wait until I'm ready to go. Talk about class. Only the rich can get away with something like that. Imagine making someone wait outside in all kinds of weather until you're ready to go. I think I'd give money to my folks. Not much. Maybe enough to buy a house or something. Despite the way they treated me, I'd still give them some money just to prove I'm a good kid. Hell, why not? Maybe I'll buy them a car as well. They're really not bad parents when I think about it, and, yet, sometimes I think they are. I think my mind has a way of hiding the truth. It makes me forget the bad stuff and remember the good, not that there was that much good. Know what else I'd buy? I think I'd buy this bar. It would be a good sound investment. There's always a need for a good bar, and when you got the best hamburger in town, you can't go wrong. Yeah, that sounds like a good idea. After all, I might not be rich forever. You know, have lots of money all the time. I'll need some kind of business to fall back on. And what better business for me could I get? I love good food, and I know my alcohol, that's for sure. Probably get married. Hope not, but you know how that goes. Some gal will want me for my money, and my other head will take over thinking for me. Happens to the best of 'em. Why not me?"

Daniels paused. He bent over the table and took a bite of his sandwich. He wiped his mouth with the back of his hand and leaned back in his chair. He was still smiling, but his eyes were now completely closed.

"Know what else?" said Daniels tilting his head back and staring with closed eyes at the ceiling. "All the important people and celebrities would want to talk to me, want to make appointments with me. Not sure why. Probably to learn how I did it. They pose as friends or colleagues just to get in to see me. They want advice from me. They need advice. They have to hold onto what they got, but don't know how. That's where I come in. I'm the answer man. I'm the one who can help them keep what they got. Only me. But they got to get through a maze of beautiful secretaries first. There would be a dozen or more secretaries who love to say no to the public and yes to me. They fight to get the honor of being alone with me. For the most part, I'm pretty generous with my time for these lovely creatures. I, usually, only have one a day, but some days, especially when it's hot like today, I might have a second one. After all, I make two women happy instead of one. Besides, it's not polite to be stingy and not share myself with beautiful women. Someone with my talents, wealth and good looks should share himself with as many women as he can. Don't you think?"

West didn't answer. He really didn't think Daniels was expecting an answer. To him, it all sounded like the musings of a drunk. John listened to what Daniels was saying but only out of respect for a friend.

Daniels opened his eyes and spread his arms out wide. "Sorry, my friend. Guess I got carried away. Damn alcohol loosens me up, and I say things I probably shouldn't."

"I understand," said West. "I guess everyone has a dream or two. Never hurts anybody to have one."

"I know I got my share of dreams," said Daniels. "I'm sure none of them will ever come true. Guess that's why they call 'em dreams."

West gulped his beer. "Guess you're right."

"What about you?" asked Daniels. "What dreams do you have?"

West's face flushed. "Oh, I don't know," he said forcing a grin. "Never expected much out of life, so I guess I never believed much in dreams."

"Come on, now. I spilled my guts, and you're just as drunk as I am."

"Come to think about it, I guess I always did have one dream."

Daniels took a bite from his sandwich and leaned forward. "Tell me. What was it?"

"I always wanted to fly," said West with a sheepish grin.

Daniels sat straight. "Hell, that ain't no big deal. A lot of guys want to fly. They call 'em pilots."

"No, not that kind of flying. I'm talking about flying, the kind of flying you do by flapping your arms."

"But that's crazy," said Daniels. "Ain't nobody ever done that before."

"I'm talking about real dreams, the kind you have when you're asleep. All the time when I was a kid, I would dream about flying, most every night too."

"Can't say as I ever dreamed about that," said Daniels. "Sounds crazy to me."

"I could soar over houses and look down on towns below. Funny thing was, nobody could see me. I would swoop down right over their heads, and they wouldn't even know it."

"Kinda like being invisible," added Daniels.

"Yeah, I suppose you're right. Except I always wanted to be invisible so I could go into the girls' locker room."

Daniels laughed. "I got to believe that every guy has had that dream."

"Seemed like any time someone was mean to me or wanted to fight, all I had to do was flap my arms and away I would go. Nobody could hurt me. Even if I didn't like what someone was saying, all I had to do was flap my arms. Funny thing is they were never offended. They just walked away. My mom and dad fought all the time when I was a little kid. I hated it. It was if it never stopped. I think that's when I first started my flying dreams. When I got a little older, I still dreamed about flying, but I dreamed I was in one of those hot air balloons floating over the countryside and houses. Nobody could touch me, nobody could hurt me. It was just me, and I was flying along like a bird. Then when I went into the joint, it seemed like that's all I did was dream about flying, except it wasn't in a balloon. I was back to flappin' my arms like when I was little. Dreamed it all the time, night and day. Got so bad, I sometimes wondered if I could come back from one of those dreams. There were times I thought I was gonna get stuck in one of the dreams and not be able to come back. Now that I think about it, it wouldn't have been all that bad being stuck in a place where I can fly away...fly away from all my problems. I always looked at heaven as a place like that. A place where you fly above everything looking down on the people and things that caused you problems and heartaches. I want to go there someday to fly above it all. Can't you feel it? Can't you feel the freedom and wonder of it all?"

"Hold on there, boy," said Daniels. "We don't want you going to heaven just yet. We got some banks to rob before you do."

West finished his hamburger and gulped his beer. He forced a grin once again. "Sounds a bit crazy, doesn't it? Wanting to fly and all. I suppose if a head doctor heard all that, he'd have me locked up for sure."

"A head doctor would have a field day with the likes of us," said Daniels.

"No self respecting doctor would be seen with the likes of us," said West.

"Let's have one more beer, and then go find another filling station. What do you say?"

"Sounds good, and this time we score big."

The sun was just setting when they parked the car next to a small neighborhood filling station. The heat was unbearable as it radiated from the pavement, so West parked in a patch of weeds in an abandoned lot next to the filling station. Daniels found a six pack on the floor in the back of the car. The beer was nearly too warm to drink, but by then they were too intoxicated to notice or even care.

A young man not even out of his teens stood at the back of a car filling it up with gas. For the next hour, they watched the young man like some animal stalking its prey. It was still too early. Cars were still stopping. However, as the evening wore on, the cars became less frequent until it was most certain they had stopped coming all together.

It was about closing time for the filling station when Daniels and West finished the warm beer. They got out of the car, pulled their guns and staggered to the front door. The young man was in the process of closing the station when they barged in the front door. They stood facing the boy, their guns waving frantically back-and-forth.

"This is a stick up," said Daniels, slurring each word.

The boy thrust his hands in the air.

"Give me your money," said Daniels.

The boy opened the cash drawer and pulled out a wad of bills. He handed it to Daniels who snatched it from his hands. Daniels thumbed through the bills to get an idea how much was there.

"Is there anymore?" asked Daniels. "You had to have done more business than this."

The boy pointed at the floor behind the counter. "There's a hole in the floor that leads to a safe. I stuff money in there from time to time."

Daniels stepped behind the counter and examined the hole. "Maybe we could dig up the safe."

The boy gave a taunting but short laugh. "That safe is buried in about a ton of concrete. I'd say you boys are out of luck."

John West turned and looked at the boy. His blood-shot eyes opened wide; his teeth bared as if he were an animal about to attack. "There he goes again," he said pulling a blackjack from his pocket. "He's making fun of us again. I told you once before not to laugh at us, you son-of-a-bitch."

West staggered across the floor and lunged at the boy, who was over a foot taller than his attacker. John swung his blackjack at the boy's head, who, by then, had ducked and instinctively covered his head with his arms. The blow errantly glanced off his shoulder. West became even more irritated. He swung his weapon again, but the boy moved causing West to miss all together. In frustration, West struck at his mid section hitting his ribs and causing the boy to buckle and drop to his knees in pain. The boy now grabbed his chest exposing his head to his attacker. West smiled. Not only was the boy's head exposed, but also it was chest-high, an easy target even for someone as inebriated as West was. He pulled back his blackjack ready to strike when Daniels grabbed John's arm.

"What the hell is the matter with you?" asked Daniels.

"The son-of-a-bitch is at it again. He's laughing at us."

"You dumb shit. That was the guy last night who was laughing at us."

West stopped struggling against Daniels grip. "Well, didn't this kid laugh at us?"

Daniels turned to the boy who was still holding his chest with both arms and was wincing in pain. "What makes the difference? I think you broke a rib or two, so the kid paid the price whether he laughed at us or not."

"I still want to crack open his melon," said West struggling to free his arm.

Daniels pulled West away from the boy. "Come on. Let's get out of here."

Chapter **Eight**

Phyllis Niebel finished with her hair and set the brush on the counter. She studied herself in the mirror until she was finally satisfied with the results. Instinctively, she swept her hands over her full-length cotton dress to eliminate any unseen wrinkles.

It was Wednesday; a day she would normally be at her job at the Ohio Textile Products, but this Wednesday was different. She had requested the day off, so that she could go with her boyfriend, Raymond, on a daylong date. For weeks, they had planned a trip to the beach at Lake Erie, which was less than a two-hour drive from their house. It was a perfect day for it. There wasn't a cloud in the sky, and the temperature promised to soar into the nineties once again.

Phyllis grabbed a small, soft-sided bag and packed her swimsuit, sunglasses, suntan lotion, and sandals for walking on the hot sandy beach. She then packed two beach towels, one for her and one for Raymond, who would without any doubt in her mind forget to bring one. She zipped up the bag, grabbed a blanket to lay on the beach and headed downstairs.

"Good morning, Mother," she said, her voice ringing with excitement.

Nolana was standing at the stove turning a pancake over in a skillet. "Good morning," said her mother, her voice short and without expression. "How did you sleep?"

Phyllis set her bag on a chair and took a seat at the table. "I finally fell asleep after it cooled down a bit."

"Maybe it wasn't the heat. Maybe you were just excited."

"That could very well be, Mother," she said. Her whole face seemed to glow. "Raymond and I have planned this for weeks. It's the first time we've ever gone away for a day."

"I know, and it bothers me very much," she said, scooping the pancake from the skillet and dropping it on a plate. She then took the plate and a bottle of syrup and set it in front of Phyllis.

"I just don't understand," said Phyllis. "When Loyal and Russ were teenagers, they got to go places."

"It's different with boys. Besides, they were off to the war when they were your age."

"Please don't forbid me to go, Mother. This means a lot to me. Besides, I'm not getting any younger. I'm almost twenty-one and still not married."

"That's another thing that bothers me," she said taking a seat across from her daughter. "I know I shouldn't pry, but do you love Raymond?"

"Why, of course I do."

"Are you sure?"

"Why do you ask, Mother?"

"I'm just worried that you might be making a mistake."

"What kind of mistake?"

"I'm worried you might settle for someone you don't really love just to get married."

"Oh, Mother, it's not like that at all. Raymond and I love one another very much. Besides, we've never really discussed marriage, and he certainly hasn't asked me to marry him."

"What do you think you'll say when he does ask you?"

Phyllis paused. "Assuming he would someday ask me, I can't really say what my answer would be. After all, I'm not an old spinster yet. I'm not even twenty-one."

"Which reminds me; your birthday is coming up, and your father and I wanted to throw you a big party. After all, you only turn twenty-one once in your life."

"Oh, I don't know, Mother. It's so expensive, and most of my friends are either married or moved away."

"Well, you think about it. If not a big party, we want to at least have a nice party with just the family."

"I will…"

Before she could finish her statement, there was a rapping on the front door.

"That must be Raymond," said Phyllis grabbing her bag and blanket and racing across the room. "See you later, Mother."

It was nearly a two-hour trip from Mansfield to Lake Erie. It wasn't necessarily a trip of a great number of miles as it was a trip down the back roads of the Ohio farm country. Such a trip could be agonizingly slow for most drivers especially ones with a schedule to keep. For Raymond and Phyllis, however, it was a pleasurable drive filled with excitement and beauty. They both loved one another's company and loved the rich farmlands as well.

They stopped at a picnic area and beach called East Harbor. Located on a small peninsula that jutted out into Lake Erie, it was an ideal spot for tourists and lovers of marine life. For two people who lived in the landlocked farmlands of corn, soybeans, and wheat, the awesome beauty of the bluish-green waves lapping over and seemingly disappearing into the white sandy beach was not only mesmerizing to them but an exhilaration as well.

Excitedly, they grabbed their bags and blanket and headed for the brightly colored beach houses that stood at the edge of the beach. After quickly changing into their swimsuits, they started hand-in-hand across the sand to stake out a spot not too close to the water that they would get wet from the spray but close enough to enjoy the sometimes crashing waves.

Since it was a weekday and most men were working at their jobs, the beach was populated with just a few women and their children who had slipped away for a little fun and to cool off in the water.

Raymond spread the blanket over the sand, and they both sat down. Raymond was a big man over six feet tall with lean strong muscles earned by working in a steel mill. He moved to Mansfield shortly after Phyllis graduated, they met and have been seeing one another ever since. Raymond's goals and ambitions were to succeed in the steel mill and move up the corporate ladder as far as he could possibly go. He also planned to get married and have a family. Raymond was a simple, uncomplicated man with realistic and attainable goals. He was good to Phyllis largely due to the fact that he was taught at an early age to respect all women and when necessary protect them even if it would put his own life in jeopardy.

It was nearly noon when Raymond came out of the water after a quick dip to cool off and sat down beside Phyllis. Friendly pleading did no good in his bid to persuade her to join him.

Raymond ran a towel through his hair. "Baffles me why you women want to go to the beach but won't go in the water."

"This won't be the last time you'll have problems understanding us," she said with an impish grin. "Besides, men are not supposed to understand us; you're only supposed to love us."

Raymond stretched out on the blanket and closed his eyes. "I need a nap," he muttered.

"No, Raymond," said Phyllis. "I want to talk."

He sat back up. "Talk about what?"

"I don't know. Tell me about your childhood."

"What do you want to know?"

Phyllis glanced at the waves crashing against the beach. "Tell me about your father."

Raymond smiled. "My dad was the greatest man who ever lived."

"You used the term, was."

"He's gone now," said Raymond.

"I'm sorry," said Phyllis. "So, tell me. What was he like?"

"My dad was probably the most caring man in the world. To look at him you would never guess it. He was a very unassuming person or so it would seem. He was very polite and quiet. He hardly spoke to us, his own family, and never would he talk to others, but when there was a tragedy or when someone needed help, he was there.

"Dad loved to travel and see the sights. He only got two weeks of vacation every year, so we would spend just about the entire two weeks traveling around the country. We didn't have much money and certainly couldn't afford to stay in a hotel, so we would find a spot in the woods or along side a road and sleep the night in a tent. I don't know why, but that was a rugged way to travel, but it certainly made great memories.

"This one particular summer, we were traveling across the western part of the country. This one day, it started raining. It started in the morning, and as the day wore on, it only got worse. Dad sensed that this was not a normal rain and could easily become a disaster. I remember that he stopped the car and got out. I didn't know at the time what he was doing but soon guessed that he was searching for any high ground. He got back in the car, and I was shocked at how soaked he was in such a short time. He began driving down a back road. It was muddy with standing water. I'm surprised we never got stuck, but within a short time I could see that we were soon heading uphill. Dad was trying to get us to the safety of high ground. I remember that we would never have made it if it hadn't been for the fact that had recently lined the road with stone. That was the only thing that saved us. If it hadn't been for that, our car would never have made it.

"Dad stopped about halfway up that mountain. There was a small clearing with plenty of room. At that height we knew we would be safe. We were sitting in the car kinda relaxing when suddenly my mother screamed. She was pointing down at the river below us. A little girl had floated away on a raft of some kind, and it was stuck against a tree. We could hear her crying all the way up where we were. We could see her mother along side of the river, her arms reaching out as if she could grab her. It was a horrible sight. I felt so bad, but what could we do?

"Then, it happened. Without saying a word, Dad was out of the car. He slid practically all the way down the side of that mountain. Now Dad was a strong man and a great swimmer, but the current of that river was almost more than he could take. He swam out into the middle of that river and rested as the current drove him towards that little girl. He regained enough energy to grab the child and started for the shore. Unfortunately, the river had other plans for him. With all his energy, he swam towards the shore still holding the girl above the water. As the water pulled him downstream, the mother followed along on the banks of the river. It looked as if Dad could see that she was losing ground, so he made a last ditch effort to get to her. I had gotten out of the car to see better and was the only one to witness my father handing the young girl to her mother. I will never forget that moment in time. I can only imagine how he must have felt knowing that he saved that little girl's life.

"It was if the river had granted him that one particular moment, because just as soon as she was safe in her mother's arms, the river jerked him away. We found his body several miles downstream. There aren't that many people who would give their life for another, but I'm absolutely positive that Dad knew what his chances of survival were. He knew upfront he wouldn't survive, but he did all the same."

Phyllis wiped her eyes. "That's one of the most touching stories I ever heard."

Raymond stretched back out on the blanket.

"What are you doing?"

"I'm going to take a nap."

"I thought we were going to talk."

"We will," he muttered. "Just as soon as I get some sleep. You think about what you want to talk about, and we'll do it for sure."

Phyllis stared at him in frustration. Something just didn't seem right. It didn't seem that they were making any progress in their relationship. Nothing new ever happened. No commitments were ever made. A future together was never discussed.

"Do you love me, Raymond?" she asked with a soft voice.

"Huh?"

"Do you love me?"

"Of course, I do," he mumbled. "Now, where was I?"

"Raymond, we've been together for a long time now."

"Uh, huh."

"Raymond...Raymond!"

"Raymond sat up. "What?"

"It just seems like our relationship is not going anywhere."

"Really? I thought we were getting along pretty good."

"We get along just fine. What I'm talking about is our future together. We don't even talk about if we have a future together."

Raymond gave her a patronizing smile. "I'll tell you what. This Sunday, we'll pack a picnic lunch and take off. We'll find a secluded spot and talk. How's that sound?"

"Phyllis paused, then smiled. "Sounds great," she said. "And I can make us chicken and potato salad, and…"

Raymond stretched back out on the blanket and went to sleep."

Chapter Nine

JULY 9, 1948: It was another day of temperatures reaching into the nineties with no relief in sight. The hot, torrid temperatures had already taken its toll. Farmers were losing livestock and crops at an alarming rate. The lush green grasses of neighborhood lawns had turned to amber and were brittle to the touch. The only thing green, by then, was the thistle and ivy that boldly sprouted in the now barren grounds.

By nightfall, the temperature slowly inched its way down a few degrees. John West and Robert Daniels found themselves in Joe's Grill and Bar, drinking and discussing such matters as the economy, the state of the world now that the war was over, and many issues of a more personal nature.

As the evening progressed, Daniels was enthusiastically involved in the conversation, but he also kept one eye on the employee at the cash register collecting payments from the customers.

Daniels gulped his beer and set the half-empty bottle on the table. "How long have we been sitting here?"

"I don't know," said West with a surprised look. "Why?"

Daniels glanced at his watch. "We've been here for four hours, and nobody has picked up the extra cash from that register."

West turns to see the register, which is near the front door. "Really?"

"I'll bet there's close to a thousand dollars in that till right now."

"You're not thinking…"

"Yes, I am."

"But I like the food in here."

"We can find another place."

West scratched his head. "I still can't believe it."

"Doesn't it seem dangerous to have the cash register near the front door? It just seems like anybody could grab the money and run."

"Is that what we're going to do?"

"As long as everybody cooperates, nobody will get hurt."

West picked up his beer and held it in the air. "Mind if I finish this?"

Daniels smiled. "Now that I think about it, let's have another one. After all, it's all on the house tonight."

It was nearly ten o'clock when Daniels finished his beer. His eyes were blurry from the alcohol. He lost count of the number of beers he had drunk. West's head nodded as he fought sleep.

"Hey, we gotta sober up," said Daniels with a firm but muted voice.

West jumped. "What's the matter?"

"We got to sober up if we're going to hit this place."

West sat up in his chair. "Sure…okay."

Daniels pushed his empty plate and bottles to the edge of the table.

"Did you ever stop and think about the fact that we never wear masks or make an attempt to hide our identity?"

West thought for a moment. "I didn't know we were supposed to."

"All thieves and robbers hide their faces, but not us. Now why is that?"

"I don't know, Robert, but I'm sure you'll tell me."

"I think it's because deep down we know we're gonna get caught. That's the way it goes for guys like us. There's no escaping it, so why fight it?"

West stared at Daniels in disbelief. "How can you say that?"

"It's easy because we're losers. We were born losers, we grew up as losers and we'll die losers. Not everybody can wear fancy clothes and have lots of money. That's just the way it is. All my life I've been a loser. I didn't want to be. Every kid in school made fun of me. Seemed like no matter what I did it was never good enough. Funny thing is everybody has something they're good at. They know it from the get-go. After all, they were born with it. Some are good at music some at painting pictures. Some are natural born leaders, and others are good at following orders. The important thing is they were born with a talent, and they recognized it at an early age. Can't say as I believe in God, but if I did, I'd say he gives everyone something special, and what you do with it is up to you. I can't help but wonder if it upsets God when you don't do anything with that talent. It's got to be a sure fired certainty that it would make him happy if you do the best with that talent. For me, it's different. God must have dozed off when I was made, at least, when they were giving me a talent. Who knows, maybe my talent is robbing people. Maybe that's what I was meant to do. Maybe that was the talent God gave me. Maybe He wants me to live a life of crime. You gotta have bad guys and losers, you know. Makes the good guys feel better about themselves. Hey, that's it. That's our talent, my friend. We were put on this earth to make the good guys feel better about themselves. They take one good look at losers like us, and immediately their egos soar. Doesn't seem fair though. We should get some kind of a break when we die. Since we succeeded at what God built us for, we should get into heaven. Of course, that wouldn't be right either. Since we're losers, we shouldn't successively get into heaven. Good God, what a paradox."

West stared at Daniels with a bewildered look. "A pair of what?"

"Never mind, my hapless friend," said Daniels. "Right now, it's time to settle our bill."

Daniels pulled out his gun and held it at his side. "Let's go."

The two men got to their feet and slowly walked across the room. Despite the late hour, most of the tables were occupied. Many were finishing their meals, others nursing drinks and discussing the day's events. It was the end of a day not only for the bar but for its patrons as well.

Daniels and West walked to the counter. It was a young girl not even out of her teens standing behind the cash register. She smiled at the men but soon sensed that something was wrong. Their faces were expressionless, almost like stone. She glanced at their hands. Neither was carrying a bill to be paid.

The smile left her face. Her good common sense told her she was in danger. She started to call for help when Daniels lifted his gun and pointed it at her.

"Give me all your money," he said his voice soft but firm. Without saying a word, she opened the register and dug rolls of bills from the till. She handed Daniels the money. His hand was steady as he took the money from her and stuffed it into his coat pocket. "Now give me what's under the till." She lifted the till from the register and grabbed a handful of bills that were twenties and higher denominations. At the same time, a middle-aged couple got in line behind West and Daniels. They were bickering about the bill and the fact that he had too much to drink. The woman sensed something was wrong and leaned over to see if her suspicions were true. She watched as the girl handed Daniels a roll of money.

"Oh, my God!" said the woman and backed away from the counter.

Daniels turned. The room grew silent as everyone watched the man and woman cautiously backing away from the two men. Some whispered to others as they realized that a robbery was in progress. A feeling of panic spread throughout the restaurant. Near the rear of the room, a big man got to his feet and slowly started walking towards them.

Daniels fired two rounds into the floor. There were screams. People scooted their chairs away from the men until they were all huddled against the back wall. The big man returned to his seat.

"Everybody just stay in your seats, and nobody will get hurt," said Daniels.

He filled his pockets with the rest of the money and started to leave. Then it came to him. It came like an inspiration. He turned and looked at all the people. They were cowering from him. Cowering from Robert Murl Daniels. It was a grand sight. He smiled as he surveyed the room. It felt good. It felt like nothing he had ever known before. He wanted to fire another round just to heighten the panic in the room. Robert Murl Daniels was in control. All these people would have to obey and do whatever he commanded. For the first time, he felt like an executive. He felt like a boss. Then, to his surprise, the image of his high school science class teacher, Mr. Gessler, came to his mind. He was standing in front of science class as he always did threatening discipline; threatening with his perfectly shaped, oak paddle to hit any student who misbehaved in his class. Mr. Gessler. Mr. David Gessler. He didn't deserve to be called mister, and he certainly didn't have the right to hit Daniels as many times as he did. But he was in control. He was always in control. With his paddle in his hand, people cowered.

"Come on," said West. "Let's get out of here."

Daniels took one last look at the room and dashed out the door.

The two men ran around to the side of the building and got into their car. They sped out of the parking lot and disappeared down a neighborhood street.

Daniels squirmed in his seat. "That was exhilarating," he said, his voice excited.

West purposely turned down different side streets until they were lost. "Yeah, that was somethin', all right."

"You didn't feel it?" asked Daniels, his fists clenched in front of him.

"Feel what?"

Daniels turned to West in disbelief. "I don't believe it. You didn't feel it?"

"I felt like we scored big in there."

"It wasn't about the money."

"That's funny 'cause I thought that's what we did it for."

"It was about the power, the incredible power we had in there," said Daniels, his face glowing. "Did you see them back there? There's no way they would have tried anything. No way. Even that big guy sat back down. Did you see that? He knew. He knew who was in control. No, this wasn't about the money. This was about David Gessler. Even David Gessler knew who was in control. He wasn't hitting me today. No, sir. I should have taken his paddle away from him. That's what I should have done. Better yet, I should have beaten him with his own paddle. Beat him to death! How do you like that, you bastard? How do you like your legs numb from the waist down? It's hours before the feeling comes back. Hours. Your ass hurts for a week. You can hardly sit down. And the other kids. Just one more thing to tease me about. Just one more thing. Yeah, that's what I should have done. I should have beaten the shit out of him with his own paddle. Justice would have been served, Mr. David Gessler. Justice would have been served.

West turned down a back alley. "Let's go home," he said with a timid voice.

"No, not yet," said Daniels.

"What do you want to do now?"

"We're going to hit another bar."

"What for? We got plenty of money now."

"Can't help it. Gotta do it."

"It's getting late."

"That's the beauty of bars. They're the last to close. Now turn down that next street."

It was a blue-collared neighborhood with rows of ranch houses, all the same, side-by-side. They drove for several more blocks until they came to a small grocery store that was closed, a filling station, and another block a small neighborhood bar. It was an ivy-covered brick building with a lighted sign that spelled out, "Pabst." Over the door was another sign that said, "Ambrose Grill." They parked the car in front of the bar and walked inside.

***

JULY 10, 1948: It was just after midnight, and most of the regulars had gone home for the night. The bar was quiet with an almost lazy kind of feeling. It was dimly lit with slow turning ceiling fans that seemed to lull patrons to sleep, some, into stupors.

Earl C. Ambrose had always wanted to own a bar, and not just any bar. He had lived in that neighborhood all his life and was determined that one day that particular bar would have his name on it. He had saved his money years before the war, during the war, and shortly after his release from the army, he made an offer on the place. Three years later, he was making a living from that same place. Not as much as he had hoped for, but enough to support his family.

Earl Ambrose was a happy man. He was doing what he had always wanted to do. It had been his dream to own this bar, and he felt blessed to be living his dream. Unfortunately, his wife did not share his happiness. There was something about a bar that frightened her. Over the years, she had seen the violence that can break out even in a sleepy little neighborhood place like theirs. Even though Earl was a big man and was an army veteran of the war, she knew he was vulnerable to the potential violence and secretly feared for his life.

West and Daniels walked through the front door, and everything stopped. All eyes turned to the two strangers who had dared to enter their seemingly private and exclusive club. Nearly all patrons of this bar and most other neighborhood bar were regulars. Many considered it their home away from home, and anybody else would likely have been considered an intruder.

The two men sat down in a booth close to the door. Within a moment or two, things somewhat returned to normal with only an occasional prying glance in their direction.

"These people seem edgy," said Daniels. "Let's order a beer, so they'll settle down."

"Are you sure we're alright here?" asked West. "They don't seem very friendly.

"They're just not used to getting strangers," said Daniels then patted his waistline where he kept his gun. "Besides, we have the equalizer right here."

"What happened to you at that last bar?" asked West. "You acted like you were out of your head."

"Just enjoying the moment, I guess," said Daniels. He began to smile. "Couldn't you feel it? We were in control of all those people. Some of them guys probably make ten, even twenty thousand a year, and he only spoke when I told him to. That's power, my friend."

"We can't be standing around like that," said West. "It just ain't safe."

Daniels turned his back to the room and pulled a roll of bills from his pocket. He thumbed through the corners mumbling aloud.

"How much did we get?" asked West.

"There must be seven, eight hundred dollars in here," he whispered.

"We have enough money. Let's get out of here."

"Hey, we're already here," said Daniels. "We might as well do it."

Ambrose was behind the bar washing drinking glasses and setting them on a shelf above the sink. He had noticed the two men who had entered the bar and taken a seat in the first booth. Just before the two men had entered, Ida, the only waitress still on duty, had disappeared into the kitchen to get an order of two hamburgers for table four.

Daniels thrust the wad of money into his coat pocket and pulled out his gun. "Get ready," he said.

West pulled out his pistol. "Aren't we rushing it?"

"No time like the present," he said and got to his feet.

"This is a stick up," said Daniels.

He started for the register. West stepped closer to the bar pointing his gun at Ambrose, who by then had set down his dishrag and glasses. He wanted to free his hands so that he could reach for the shotgun that he kept just under the bar. Daniels set his gun on the counter. He, then, hit the no sale key, and the drawer flew open. With one hand, he picked up the till and scooped up the currency with the other.

Just then, the heavy swinging doors that lead to the kitchen burst open, and Ida appeared carrying a tray of food. The clamor startled West. He turned and fired his weapon. The bullet hit the woman in the shoulder shattering the bone, exited out her back and lodged in the wall behind her. The tray of dishes and glasses crashed to the floor distracting West.

Ambrose quickly glanced at Daniels. His hands were still in the cash register, and his gun was still on the counter. He turned to West. Ambrose could see that he was still stunned as he watched Ida fall to the floor. He reached for the shotgun. West caught movement from the corner of his eye. He turned and fired. The bullet crashed through Ambrose's skull. It lacerated through the brain shredding the soft gray matter, nearly cutting it in half from the concussion. As it penetrated the other side of his head, it ruptured a hole that blew away nearly half the side of his head. Like so much dead weight, he fell to the floor, his head spewing blood across the room.

West was stunned as he stared at the carnage. Daniels finished stuffing the money in his pockets and grabbed West by the arm.

"Come on. Let's go," said Daniels, and they disappeared out the door.

Chapter Ten

Rex was the name of his horse, and it had pulled his wagon for over ten years. To the rest of the world, it was an oddity, but to the inmates and guards at Mansfield Reformatory it was just another day for John Niebel. Being superintendent of all the farms at the prison, John needed transportation to survey and supervise the various operations that fell under his responsibility. Early in his career, he found that a horse and buggy was economical, mobile, and provided a little extra fertilizer for the growing fields.

It was another hot day, and John was inspecting the cornfields. The hot summer sun had destroyed many of the beans and some of the gardens, but field corn was different. Grown solely for feeding livestock, field corn was tough and durable. Able to survive on the smallest amounts of water, it could endure the hottest of seasons and just about anything else that nature could throw at it.

John stopped the horse and got down from his rig. He walked over to the edge of the cornfield and pulled back the husk on a randomly chosen stalk of corn. Farmland used for growing crops has fertile areas capable of producing large and plentiful harvests, and has other areas that produce less than acceptable yields. Lower lying grounds are susceptible to flooding which will kill just about any crop.

Satisfied with the condition of the first ear of corn, John stepped over to another stalk. He grabbed an ear and started to pull back the husk, when suddenly he felt dizzy, his head reeling in a circle. His feet stuttered as he tried to keep his balance. Then, the bright light that had been flashing off and on in his eyes went dark. He whirled almost gracefully in a circle and fell backwards onto the soft, tilled soil.

An inmate saw John fall and ran to his side. He knelt down, carefully picked up his upper torso and cradled his head in his arms. Guards and inmates alike rushed to the scene, many offering assistance of any kind. Two of the guards were personal friends of John and were aware that he had a bad heart.

Then, as quickly as he had fallen, his eyes popped open and he sat up.

"What happened?" he asked. His voice was a bit raspy.

"You blacked out," said one of the guards. "Come on, John, let's get you to the hospital."

"No, I'm alright," said John struggling to his feet.

"John, we both know you have a bad ticker," said the guard. "You need to see a doctor."

By then, John was on his feet and had regained his balance. "I think the heat got to me. That's all."

"If you won't go to the hospital, then I'm taking you home," said the guard. "You can, at least, take the rest of the day off."

"I won't argue with that," said John.

In all the years Nolana Niebel was married to John, she had never known him to take a sick day, skip work or come home early. Not only did he love his job, but he was steadfast in his devotion to it as well. Obviously, it came as a shock to her when two men escorted John through the front door in the middle of the afternoon.

"Are you alright?" she asked rushing to his side.

"I'm fine," said John. "Just a little dizzy, that's all."

"Don't let him kid you," said one of the guards. "He went down like a sack of potatoes." They turned to leave. "Take care of him, Mrs. Niebel, and make him stay home if he's going to pass out like that. We haven't got time to haul him home," he said with a smile.

John sat on the sofa and leaned back. Nolana sat on a chair near the sofa.

"What happened?" she asked.

"The heat got to me. That's all. I'll be fine."

"I worry about you, John. You work too much and need to slow down."

"Now, Nolana, don't make more of this than there is. I'm not the first to be overcome by the heat."

"You worry me, John. It's not normal to work as many hours as you do."

"I just read in the paper where there have been nearly sixty people die from the heat so far this year," he announced.

"Well, today, you're going to rest," she said. That place will just have to get along without you."

John took a deep breath. "I'll have to admit that I'm looking forward to our vacation."

"I can't tell you how excited I am about getting away for a while."

"Are we still having a birthday party for Phyllis?" asked John.

"The plans are all set."

"Looks like August should be a good month for us."

Nolana took his hand. "I love my life with you," she said. "I really do."

John kicked up his feet and stretched out on the couch. "And I love my life with you."

"I thank God for all He's given us and the life we have together."

John yawned and closed his eyes. "God has been good to us. That's for sure."

It was nearly five in the afternoon when John was awakened from his nap by a commotion at the back door. Before he could get to his feet, through the door walked his neighbor and co-worker, Red Harris.

"What some people won't do to get out of work," said Harris with a grin.

"How are you, Red?"

"I'm fine," said Harris. "More importantly, how are you?"

"The sun got to me. That's all."

"Word is your old ticker was the problem."

"Good grief," said John. "They're worse than a bunch of old women."

"Some of the guys are concerned about you."

"I'm fine," said John. "Just needed a little rest. That's all."

"Well, it's good to hear that you're doing okay. Anything I can do for you, just let me know."

"That's real nice of you, Red, but I should be back to work tomorrow."

"By the way, the state police have been asking around. Seems that two of our parolees shot and killed a bar owner in Columbus. The two guys were John West and Robert Daniels. Remember either of them?"

John thought for a moment. "Not that I recall."

"The reason I asked is that West worked on the farm," said Harris.

John paused. "Doesn't ring a bell."

"Well, I remember that Daniels," said Harris. "He was such a smart ass. I should have taken care of him when I had the chance."

"Sounds like he needed his ass kicked."

"I roughed him up more than a couple times. Didn't do no good. There's only one thing to do with the likes of him. Yes, sir. Guys like him need to be taken care of, if you know what I mean. Mark my words. He's gonna hurt somebody, maybe worse. I've seen that look before, maybe only once or twice, but you don't soon forget it. It's in his eyes. If you look straight into his eyes, you'll see evil. It's like looking into the eyes of the devil himself."

John forced a grin. He felt uncomfortable listening to his friend, almost frightened. "Red, I don't believe I ever heard you talk like this."

"Don't believe I ever dealt with anybody like that Daniels fella. He's pure evil. Ain't ashamed to tell you that I plan on keepin' my doors locked. Yes, siree. Wouldn't put it past him to come back here to get me, and if he got the drop on me there's no tellin' what he might do. Makes you wonder how he and his kind got that way. I'll bet he had hard working parents who raised him proper too. Guys like him were born that way. I don't think God wants everybody to be alike. He wants there to be a variety of people, different kinds so we don't get bored with one another. I just don't see why He would put somebody like Daniels on the earth. I suppose He has his reasons, but it just don't seem right."

John cleared his throat. "I've never seen you so worked up."

"You would too, John, if you had looked into the devil's eyes. I don't know anything about this West fella, but my guess is he's no better than Daniels."

"Did you hear what happened there in Columbus?"

"All I know is they was robbin' a bar, and something went wrong. They ended up killing a guy and wounding a woman. Don't know which one done it. Guess it don't really matter, 'cause one's guilty as the other."

"Matters to me," said John. "Takes a real special person to drop the hammer on another human and I want to know who that person was."

"Well, suppose I should be gettin' on home. The missus will be wondering where I am." Harris walked to the front door and stopped. He turned and looked out a window. "You know, if you were to keep that shade up, you could watch the coming and goings at my house, and I could watch yours. That way, I got your back, and you got mine."

John got to his feet and started across the floor. He was a bit unsteady but got stronger with each step. "Sounds like a plan, my friend. Thanks for the tip. We keep the doors locked at nights on a regular basis, but we'll be extra cautious."

John stood there on the porch long after his friend had driven away.

Chapter Eleven

It was the early morning of July 10th. John West twisted the knob of the car radio hoping to find a clear station. He and his companion, Robert Daniels hoped to hear a broadcast of the news to see if the shooting death of Charles Ambrose was worthy of statewide or even a national attention. They were lost somewhere in the farmlands of southern Ohio and nowhere near a city where a radio station's broadcast could be heard.

Since they had taken no precautions by hiding their identity, it was fairly certain to the two men that the authorities must have already identified them as Ambrose's killers and quite possibly had linked them to the other crimes they had committed.

They decided to flee the state. Even if they achieved national recognition for their crimes, their notoriety would be more or less confined to the state of Ohio. Residents of neighboring states would have a passing interest and quite possibly would read the gruesome details of the Ambrose murder, but would feel less threatened than the people of Ohio and, in particular, the people of Columbus, Ohio. They could travel about undetected and free to live guarded if not normal lives.

They drove on throughout the day, until exhausted and hungry they stopped in Nashville, Tennessee. They stayed there for nearly a week in a small, run-down motel near the edge of town. They checked newspapers and listened to the radio, and satisfied that their crimes had not reached the national media, they packed up and drove part of the way back home.

***

JULY 16, 1948: It was early evening when they stopped at a motel in Lexington, Kentucky. They checked in and headed for a bar just across the road. Even though the sun was setting, the temperature was still hovering around a hundred degrees.

Inside the bar, large ceiling fans turned slowly setting a lazy mood but doing little to cool the place. It was a slow night as was all Tuesday nights; only a few tables and booths were occupied. A large man with rolled up sleeves and massive tattooed-arms swabbed the inside of drinking glasses with a once clean white towel. Slow, intoxicating music played on a radio, and a middle-aged couple leaned on one another as they slowly shuffled around the dance floor.

West and Daniels entered the front door, ordered two beers and sat down in a booth near the rear of the room.

"I think it's time we went back to Columbus," said Daniels.

"Aren't you afraid of getting caught?" asked West.

"We know it didn't go national, and if it did make the state news, it's probably back page stuff by now."

"How 'bout someplace other than Columbus?"

"Naw, we'll be alright. After all, the people in the places we go could care less."

"Where are we going next?" asked West.

Daniels' eyes fell on two young girls sitting at a booth one the other side of the room. They were whispering to one another and laughing hysterically, and it was the second time Daniels had caught them smiling directly at them.

"We're going to get laid, that's where we're going," said Daniels still staring at the girls.

West turned around to see what had mesmerized his friend.

"We don't need them," said West turning back and staring at the floor.

The bartender slid two beers across the table and returned to his work.

"What are you talking about? I don't know about you, but it's been a long time for me."

West turned and looked once again. Both girls were staring at them and talking softly to one another.

"I don't think so," he muttered.

"Good God, man," said Daniels. "They're practically begging us to give it to them. Let's ask them over here."

"No, please don't."

"Why not?"

"I'm afraid. That's why not."

"Afraid of what?"

"Just afraid."

"Do you think they're going to steal our money?"

"No."

"Then what are you afraid of?"

"Look at me," said West. "I'm ugly. Girls don't want to go out with me. All they've ever done is make fun of me. I just don't need that in my life."

"You just haven't found the right girl, Johnnie. Haven't you heard the saying that for everyone there is someone? You just haven't found her. That's all."

"Well, I can tell you right now, that someone ain't over there."

"How do you know unless you try?"

"They're too pretty."

"What's that got to do with anything?"

"No pretty girl is going to have anything to do with me. She's going to have to be a dog like me."

Daniels grabbed his beer and got to his feet. "Come on. Let's go over there. Just relax. Everything will be okay."

West reluctantly got to his feet and followed him across the room.

"You girls want some company?" asked West.

"Sure, sit down," said one of the girls.

"My name is Robert, and this here is Johnnie."

"I'm Betty Jo, and this is Peggy."

"You girls live around here?" asked Daniels.

"We live on the other side of town," said Betty.

"What are you doing all the way over here? Has to be a bar over on your side of town," asked Daniels.

Betty gulped down the rest of her beer and belched. Both girls laughed hysterically.

"We come over here when we're in the mood for some action," said Betty.

"Well, what a coincidence," said Daniels. "We're in the mood for some action ourselves."

"What about your friend here?" asked Betty. "He don't seem to be in the mood for anything."

"You see, Johnnie here just lost his mother, and he's feelin' a bit down."

Peggy reached across the table and took West's hand. "I'm sorry, Johnnie. Is there anything I can do?"

West gave Daniels a quick glance. "I'll be fine."

"Actually, we came in here hoping to find someone to show him a good time. You know...help to forget."

Betty grabbed Daniels' beer and drank it down. "Five beers ago, we'd have told you guys to get lost, but right now, you guys look real fine. Got a place around here?"

"Right across the road," said Daniels.

"Get us a bottle, and let's go have some fun," said Betty.

***

JULY 17, 1948: The late morning sun streamed through the slatted blinds sending hazy, muted light across the room. Daniels sat up in bed and glanced around the room. Betty was naked and still asleep. West and Peggy were asleep as well, their legs and arms intertwined. He had suspected that West was still a virgin, and, from what he had heard and seen the night before, he was more certain than ever. However, Daniels was pleasantly surprised how quickly he learned and was able not only to satisfy himself but take care of Betty as well. Obviously, she must have taught him a few things, things that were instructional as well as self-indulgent.

Daniels gently nudged West until he was awake. The two men got dressed and slipped out the front door.

"Come on," said Daniels. "Let's get out of here."

"Without the girls?" asked West.

"Of course."

"Let's take 'em with us."

"You can't be serious."

"I think I'm in love with Peggy."

"That's just great," said Daniels. "Your first piece of ass, and you're in love."

"She's not my first."

"Who was then?"

"My cousin showed me a thing or two back in the first grade."

"That doesn't count for two reasons. First, it happened before puberty, and, second, it was your cousin. Cousins don't count."

"I still want to bring her along."

"Hell, she doesn't even look like she's fourteen."

"She's seventeen."

"That's jail bait."

West snorted. "After what we did to that bar owner, having sex with a minor is small potatoes."

"Alright," said Daniels. "Wake 'em up, and let's get out of here."

It was midafternoon when they checked in at a small motel near Daniels' old neighborhood. It seemed a bit risky, but

Daniels wanted to experience the excitement of staying in the same area where law enforcement officers were diligently searching for him. Besides, if they needed anything, they could send the girls out.

Daniels spread a newspaper over one bed. There was nothing about the shooting on the front page. He opened it up. Nothing on the second page. His eyes turned to the third page. There it was. A small story about the as-of-yet unsuccessful manhunt for Daniels and West.

"Well, at least they spelled our names right," said Daniels.

West leaned over his shoulder to read the story. "So we made the news."

Betty leaned over his other shoulder. "You guys killed a man?"

"Hey, he was reaching for a shotgun," said West.

"I can't believe we're running from the law," said Betty. "That makes us about as guilty as you two."

Peggy gulped down a beer and set the empty bottle on a nightstand. "Lighten up," she said. "I'm sure it was self-defense."

"Yeah, it was self-defense," said West. "If I hadn't shot him first, he'd a done us in."

Betty slowly sat on the edge of the bed. "I can't believe this is happening. I just thought we were out for a good time."

"We are," said Daniels. "It was a little problem we had before we met you two."

"Seems a little dangerous for us to be around here, don't you think?" asked West.

"We should lay low for now," said Daniels. "I just want to check out the newspapers, and then we'll get out of town."

***

JULY 19, 1948: It was late morning when they loaded the car and sped out of town. They decided to drive to a small town just outside Detroit, Michigan called Flat Rock. Betty had a sister there, and it seemed like the perfect place to hide for a while.

Daniels was driving and soon found himself on country roads on his way to Michigan. Seemed the safest way to travel. There always was the possibility of roadblocks on the major highways. The others were asleep, and Daniels resisted the temptation to turn on the radio.

Daniels' fears were right. Not only were the officials actively looking for them, the search had become so big that the papers referred to it as a "massive manhunt." Because of the number of investigators assigned to the case and the number of patrol officers trying to help by searching for leads and evidence, the local police force was stretched nearly beyond its limits. The state police were called in as well and every trained investigator was assigned to the case even if they already had an assignment. No stone was left unturned. It looked as if it was an all out effort to catch two men. It was as if someone had declared war on an enemy that consisted of two men. It just didn't seem right; all this fuss over a bar owner. The guy probably wasn't what one would describe as a model citizen anyhow; probably cheated on his taxes. Probably didn't go to church either. Hell, he made a living pandering alcohol to the public. It wasn't like they shot him with no provocation. The man intended to, at the very least, inflict injury on them if not mortally wound them. Whatever happened to the right of self-defense? Yeah, he had it coming to him all right. He practically asked for it, and, yet, everybody in the state was after them. People get murdered everyday, and they call out the militia. Why had this particular killing become such a colossal event? Why him? Why Robert Daniels? It had always been that way. Could never get attention from him. Tried to do what was right. Tried to get attention from him when he did the right thing, but it was never good enough. Tried to please him, make him happy. Only attention he ever got was when he was bad or did something wrong. Then he got his attention. Yeah, his father gave him plenty of attention then.

It was early afternoon when they finally arrived in Flat Rock. It was a small industrial town that prospered greatly from the generous tax subsidies of large corporations. The residential community was entirely blue-collar and stood in the shadows of the foul smelling, noisy factories. Peggy directed him down a dirt road that led to her sister's house.

Peggy's sister, Susie, had been alone since her husband was killed in the war. It had been four years since his death, and, yet, she still had not made the adjustment to life without him. Since she had no kids, the three-bedroom house provided more than enough room for the four guests. Peggy wasn't sure how her sister would react to boys and girls sleeping in the same room, so to avoid any embarrassing confrontations, they decided to have the boys room together and the girls do the same. Besides, they could always switch off in the middle of the night.

It was late at night, and Daniels and West were getting ready for bed.

"Just our luck," said Daniels. "Living with a woman who doesn't allow booze in her house."

West paused. "You know, I don't think we had a drink all day."

"This is the first time I've been sober since I got out of the pen," said Daniels.

"I'm not all that sure I like being sober."

"I guess it don't hurt to give our livers a rest."

West sat on the edge of the bed. "So, what are we going to do tomorrow?"

"I have a plan for tomorrow," said Daniels. "On the way up here, I drove by a sign somewhere in Ohio that said so many miles to Mansfield. That reminded me of a pact you and I made while we were in the pen."

"To get Red Harris."

"Exactly."

"So, is that your plan? To get Harris?"

"I figure you and I can drive down there tomorrow and take care of business."

"You want to leave the girls behind?"

"I don't think they'll want to have anything to do with this."

"Yeah, I suppose you're right," said West.

Daniels smiled and patted his friend on the back. "Tomorrow, we settle an old debt."

***

JULY 20, 1948: It was a Tuesday, and the sun was unbearably hot that day, as it had been most every day that summer. The weatherman predicted another scorching ninety degrees with a slight possibility of rain.

The boys got a late start and didn't arrive in Mansfield until early evening. The setting sun was already casting long shadows. Its day was finished, and once again it had brutally scorched the earth leaving behind a world too hot to touch.

They parked in front of a bar called the Ring Nightclub. They served drinks and had good food, but more importantly, it was a place where Harris hung out.

It was an old neighborhood bar with dim lights and quiet talk. The boys found a booth in the back and ordered hamburgers and beer. Their waitress was old with a face hardened with time. She brought a second round of beers with the food, asked if they needed anything else and disappeared into the kitchen.

"I've waited a long time for this," said Daniels taking a bite from his sandwich.

West poured ketchup on his fries. "To get Harris?"

"I want to see him squirm. I want him to experience fear like he did to us. And it's not just that. I want him to feel the indignity, the inhumanity of being bullied. I want to take his manhood away just like he did to me."

"There was another guard in there I'd like to meet up with," said West. "He used to hit me in the stomach with his stick. That way, it never showed bruises. Can't remember his name. I guess Harris will have to pay for his deeds."

Daniels gulped down his beer and set the mug on the table. "You know that bar owner we shot in Columbus was the first guy I ever saw killed. I got to tell you I'm not proud of what we done, but I got to tell you something else, I kinda enjoyed it. It was almost a God thing. For a moment there, we had control of that man's life. I'm not saying I want to kill again. In fact, I never really intended on killing Harris. I always thought I'd like to meet up with him and maybe rough him up a bit. But after watching that bar owner get his, seeing all that blood and stuff, I'm not so sure I wouldn't want to pull the trigger myself. After all, it was you who did it. You were the one who had the pleasure. I think if we're going to do Harris, it's going to be me who drops the hammer. Do you mind?"

"I don't mind," said West. "He's all yours."

Daniels scanned the bar. "Wish he'd show up right about now. I think I'd plug him from right here. He wouldn't even know what hit him."

"That sounds like a big mistake."

"Why do you say that?"

West smiled. It wasn't often he thought of something that Daniels hadn't. "I'd want him to know who it was that was dropping the hammer. I'd want him to suffer a bit before it happened. He needs to crawl on the ground and beg for his life. That's what Red Harris needs to do."

"Damn! Right on all counts," said Daniels. "I'm impressed."

"When do you want to go find him?"

"After a while. I think the best time is after everybody is in bed."

"Hate to ask this, but do you have any idea where he lives?" asked West.

"Oh, my God," said Daniels, the smile disappearing from his lips. "I have no idea. I think he lives somewhere out on Route thirteen."

"We know he lives on or near the farm."

Daniels pushed aside his beer. "We can't go door-to-door looking for him."

"I have an idea," said West. "I'm going to get a butt load of nickels and start calling all the Harris' in the book."

"You can't go calling people in the middle of the night," said Daniels. "It just ain't right."

West got to his feet. "I gotta try," he said and walked over to the bar. He bought a fistful of nickels, grabbed a phone book and returned to the table. He took a seat and opened the book. "Damn, there's a shitload of Harris's in here."

"I told you."

"What's his first name? There ain't no Red Harris in here."

"I think it's Willis, but I can't be sure."

West turned back to the book. "There's a bunch of them in here. Grab your beer and let's go over to that table by the phone."

West spent the next hour calling people with the last name of Harris. Most of his calls went unanswered, and the few calls that were answered were met with indignation.

It was nearly midnight when the two men left the bar. They were both intoxicated, and they were searching intently for something exciting to do. They got in their car and began to drive aimlessly around town. By then, West was driving, and Daniels was holding his gun in his hands, pointing it out the window and even fired one round.

A carload of black youths passed by. One of them yelled something out the window, and they all laughed.

"Let's get 'em," said West. He sped up and overtook their car forcing them to stop. They each got out of the car with guns drawn. The black youth apologized, and they fled from the scene unharmed.

It wasn't enough. It seemed only to infuriate the primal feelings they were having. They needed to somehow satisfy this incredible urge to do something exciting. They needed to find Harris. He would make the perfect target to vent these hostile feelings.

"I know how we can find Harris," blurted Daniels. "I know where the guy lives who's in charge of the farm. In fact, he's superintendent over the farm system."

"I think his name is Niebel," said West.

"That's it. Everyone called him Superintendent Niebel. Let's go."

They headed north on Route Thirteen until they were at the edge of town. Daniels ordered West to pull over and stop on the shoulder of the road. He turned on the dome light and pulled out a map to check their location. A state trooper slowly approached their car from the rear. He stopped beside their car and studied the two men. Daniels looked up and saw the markings on the car. He practically froze when he realized that it was a police officer. "Christ," he muttered aloud. He, then, smiled at the officer and slightly nodded his head as an informal greeting. With that, the trooper was satisfied that these two men were harmless and slowly drove away.

"Damn, that was close," said West.

"I think I soiled myself," said Daniels.

"Think he's gone for good?" asked West.

"Yeah, I think so."

"We should have popped him right there in his car. That's what we should have done."

"I don't think so," said Daniels. "If you think there's a lot of cops after us now, wait until you kill one. Hell hath no fury."

"Where do we go from here?" asked West.

Daniels glanced at the map. "Go straight up there to that next road and turn left."

West drove slowly following the road as it turned to the left. They parked alongside of the road just a few yards from the Niebel house for several minutes and then pulled into the driveway. It was 1:30 in the morning.

Chapter Twelve

JULY 21, 1948: The day dawned to a cloudless sky. The weatherman promised, yet, another hot day and the possibility of rain. Everything seemed right in the world. The Cleveland Indians, hot on the trail of a pennant, were in New York for a four game series. I REMEMBER MAMA was playing at the movies, and the number one hit song was WOODY WOODPECKER by Kay Kyser.

At the Mansfield Reformatory, the day shift of guards filed in the Conference Room for their daily meeting. It was already 6:30, and everyone was present except for two men. Superintendent Arthur Glattke was missing, but it was noted that he was attending a meeting of state prison officials in Cleveland. The other man who was not in attendance was Superintendent John Niebel, and the reason for his absence was unknown. In fact, in the twenty years he had been working there, he had only missed one other 6:30 meeting and had never been late. Despite his impeccable attendance record, nobody felt or expressed any real concern. John hadn't been feeling well and had even mentioned taking a day off. The guards finally settled the Niebel absence as a fifty-year-old man taking a badly needed day off.

Two hours later, next door neighbor, Willis Harris, otherwise known as Red Harris, knocked on the front door of the Niebel house. He was in the middle of a project in his basement and needed a piece of rope. He knocked again, this time a little harder. Seemed strange. They always promptly answered the door. They weren't on vacation. It was 8:30 in the morning, and, without fail, both John and Nolana always got out of bed at five every morning.

The house looked dark and empty. Harris stepped back and looked to see if any lights were on in the upstairs bedrooms. The rooms were as dark as the downstairs. He marched around to the side of the house and knocked soundly on the porch door. Still no response.

Harris was now concerned. In all the years he had known the Niebels, he had never known a time when at least one of them was home. He stepped off the porch and walked over to the two-car garage. Chances are he will find the garage empty. He opened one of the doors and to his surprise he found both John's car and the one belonging to Phyllis.

An alarm went off in Harris's head. Something was wrong. He went back to the house and tried the porch door handle. It was unlocked. He walked inside and tried the door to the house. It was unlocked as well. His hands shook as he swung the door open. He could feel his heart pounding in his chest. He so badly wanted to hear Nolana surprise him by asking him if he wanted a cup of coffee. Yet, the house was dead quiet.

Harris stepped inside the kitchen. When he did, his fears were soon confirmed. The kitchen looked as if it had been ransacked. Drawers had been pulled out, their contents strewn all over the floor. Cupboards emptied, and dishes smashed as well. This was, indeed, a surprise to Harris since Nolana was such a fastidious homemaker; nothing left out, everything in its place. Harris glanced into the dining room. On the table were two purses and a wallet with their contents spilled over the table. That was enough for him. He picked up the telephone and called the sheriff's office.

Frank Robinson had been the sheriff of Richland County for nearly twenty years. He was a big man with broad shoulders and strong arms. His face was rugged with weathered skin and a square jaw. Yet, when he laughed, his eyes disappeared into slits, and his face glowed with little-boy charm.

Frank's accomplishments as a sheriff and his nearly psychic abilities were legendary throughout the county if not the state. Very few, who committed a crime under his jurisdiction, escaped justice. It was said that he could almost sense when someone was even thinking about doing wrong.

He had a slow-talking, easy-going manner about him that deceived people into believing he was not only slow-witted but also incapable and uninterested in performing his job. His apparent ineptness and lack of enthusiasm for his job was infuriating to the victims of a crime. They couldn't imagine this man catching a criminal, until they experience his swift results and his long-standing stellar record.

Frank opened the front door of the Niebel house and stepped inside. He stood in one spot for several minutes. It was if he was trying to use his senses and his keen mind to detect any wrongdoing.

He slowly moved through the house searching for evidence that would tell him what had happened if anything. It was a big house, quiet now, strangely quiet as if it were in mourning. Frank noticed John Niebel's eyeglasses were lying on a table. Bureau and buffet drawers were open as if they had been ransacked. Cigarette butts were ground into the rugs on the first and second floors. Underclothing for each of the three missing members of the family was found in the bedrooms. Shoes and stockings were scattered on the floor. It seemed strange to him. All the evidence indicated a robbery had taken place, and, yet, jewelry was neatly lying on a dresser. He then found the wallet and purses with their contents scattered on the dining room table just as Harris had reported as well as the ransacked kitchen.

All the evidence, especially the fact that both cars were still in the garage, now suggested that the family had been kidnapped. Frank called the Federal Bureau of Investigation and asked for assistance as well as the State Highway Patrol. He then called in all his deputies to canvass the area for evidence.

It was about 10:00 in the morning when they heard from Lowell J. Snyder, a neighbor who lived across the road. He reported seeing a light-colored car in the Niebel driveway about 1:30 in the morning.

When Frank heard about the light-colored car, something clicked inside him. There was something about that light-colored car that was significant. He walked across the road and knocked on Mr. Snyder's door. He was an old man with glasses, hunched over and required the use of a cane.

"Can I help you?" he asked still standing in the doorway behind a screen door.

"My name is Frank Robinson. I'm the sheriff in these parts."

"I know you," said Snyder pointing a finger at Frank. "I seen yer picture in the papers. I done told yer deputy everything I know."

"Yes, and I appreciate your coming forward with the information like that. I really do, but I need to ask you a question or two."

"That's fine," said Snyder. "Ask away."

"You said you saw a light-colored vehicle parked in their driveway last night. Now, it had to have been awfully dark, no moon and all, could that car have been one of the Niebel's?"

"Not a chance. Both John and his daughter Phyllis have black cars...always have."

Frank scratched his head, then turned and spit on the ground. "Did you have your glasses on at the time?"

"Nope," said Snyder. "Don't need 'em. Got great eyes for seeing things at a distance. Just can't see shit close up."

"Did you happen to see what kind of car it was?"

"Looked like a Pontiac to me, but I couldn't be sure. That's why I never said anything to that deputy of yours. He told me he only wanted the facts and no guesswork. Kinda rude young fella, but sure looked like he loved his work."

"Just what exactly did you see?"

"I seen the car sittin' over there on that side road with his lights off. He was facing towards Mansfield. He sat there for nearly fifteen minutes, I suppose, and then he up and backed into the Niebel's driveway. That seemed a bit strange. I watched for another fifteen minutes and nothing happened so I went on back to bed. Another strange thing was the Niebel's porch light went on briefly, then went back off. Mrs. Niebel always turns that light on when they go to bed because of the bread man who stops at their place early in the morning."

"I want to thank you, Mr. Snyder," said Frank. "You've been a big help."

"Lowell."

"What?"

"Call me Lowell. The only Mr. Snyder I ever knew was my father."

Frank smiled. He turned to walk away and stopped. "By the way, Lowell, if you don't mind my asking, what were you doing up at that hour anyway?"

"Peeing," said Lowell. "Get up practically every hour, and I always look out the front window." I can't remember a time when I could sleep through the night without gettin' up."

Frank smiled. "It's hell getting old, ain't it?" he said and walked away.

Frank walked across the road and stood in the Niebel's front yard. It was a big house made of wood with a brick, screened-in sun porch. He walked around to the side of the house. It had a door with a screened-in porch as well.

A state trooper got out of his car and walked towards the house.

"Can I have a minute of your time?" asked Frank.

"Certainly, Sheriff," said the trooper.

"You boys have been tracking them fellers who killed that Ambrose guy in Columbus, haven't you?"

"Sure have. Why?"

"Wonder if you could tell me what you know?"

"Well, we have three eyewitnesses who identified the killers as Robert Daniels and John West. In fact, they were paroled out of your Mansfield Reformatory."

"Did they see what kind of car they were driving?"

"Yes, sir. It was a light gray Pontiac probably about ten years old."

Frank extended his hand. "Thank you, sir. You've been most helpful."

The trooper took his hand. "Don't mention it," he said and walked away.

Frank walked around to the back of the house. There were only three windows on that side of the house with a submerged door to the cellar. The backyard was larger than normal with a vast cornfield surrounding it. He turned and gazed across the head-high field of cornstalks. A gentle breeze rustled the dry, brittle leaves creating a melodic, almost mesmerizing sound.

"That's it!" he shouted to nobody in particular. "The cornfields! I knew there was something about the cornfields!"

A deputy had just got out of his car. Frank pointed at him. "Get as many men as you can and get out there in that field. I want every inch searched."

Frank walked back inside the house. The Ohio Mobile Crime Laboratory had been summoned and was busy checking for fingerprints. They were comparing the prints to the members of the Niebel family and with men discharged from the reformatory with the last eight months. However, experts from the state bureau of investigation were unable to obtain clear fingerprints, only smudges. They said the intruders evidently wore gloves.

Frank walked into the dining room. The two purses and wallet with their contents strewn across the table remained untouched. Frank poked at the items. There were lipsticks, mirrors, keys, photos, chewing gum and pieces of candy. He carefully opened one purse. There were eleven dollars in it, and a handful of change in the other. That was strange. Somebody was obviously searching for something, and, yet, left behind money.

Reformatory officials were notified, and because of John's ill health decided he might have taken seriously sick. Dr. John V. Horst of the reformatory and George Allarding, who was assistant superintendent of the guards, summoned as many men that could be spared to search the farm. They said that Niebel, in his twenty years of service at the institution, had never been involved in any difficulty. They described him as a strict disciplinarian in dealing with inmates on the farm.

Officials planned to question an inmate who was close friends with the missing farm superintendent in the hopes he might be able to supply information.

They especially wanted to learn if any threats had been made to Niebel. Officials said that they would search the whereabouts of all inmates released in the last six months.

Besides their daughter, Phyllis, John and Nolana had two sons, Russell and Loyal. Both served in the Navy during the war and were released shortly after it ended. Russ was a cook, and Loyal was an electronic technician. After reuniting at home, a discussion erupted between the two brothers as to what type of work they would pursue. Loyal advised his brother to go into electronics and in particular television. Even though television was new and the future of it seemed dim, Russ decided to take his brother's advice. He joined a radio and television repair school in Chicago and by July of 1948, after nearly two years, he was only a few months from graduation.

Twenty-four year old Loyal was the first family member to be called about the disappearance of his parents and sister. He joined the investigators at the Niebel residence to see if he could help.

Frank learned who he was and strolled over to meet him.

"Loyal Niebel?" said Frank extending his hand.

"Yes," said Loyal taking his hand.

"Sheriff Frank Robinson."

"How do you do, sir?"

"Call me Frank. That sir business was alright for the navy, but I'm just an old country sheriff."

"Fair enough...Frank."

"Sorry to meet under these circumstances. Hopefully, your family will show up unharmed. I'd like to think we overreacted and wasted a lot of taxpayers' money by being out here. Hell, I hope I get in trouble for calling out the militia over nothing."

"I just want to know that they're okay."

"Got a couple questions for you."

"Go right ahead and ask."

"Can you think of anybody who might have a grudge against your father?"

"I've been thinking about that," said Loyal. "Can't say as I ever heard him say anything like that."

"Has he had any problems at work?"

"Dad never talked about his job. Even though he was called out at all hours, he still tried his best to keep his job separate from his family."

"Don't mean to pry, and I really hate to ask this, but how did your folks get along? Did you hear them arguing much? Any problems with their marriage?"

Loyal grinned. "You're barking up the wrong tree here. I know what you're snooping for, but this is a dead alley for you. I never heard them argue once in all the years I lived there. They didn't smoke, didn't drink, went to church every Sunday, and loved one another very much."

"I'd say they were two lucky people," said Frank.

Loyal glanced at the ground. "Before today, I'd say you were right. I just hope their luck is still with them."

Frank agreed and broke away from the young man. He walked slowly to the backyard and stood near the fence gazing as if in a trance across the field of corn.

"You're hiding something from me," he muttered aloud. "I can't put my finger on it, but you're hiding something very important from me," he said, his words lost in the wind.

***

It was 2:30 in the afternoon. The sun was at its peak with temperatures in the nineties. Reverend Herbert Veler of Stoney Ridge, a former Mansfield minister, and Robert Zoeller, 18, of Chillicothe, a counselor for the Lutheran church boys' camp, were taking 65 boys on a hike. They had been gone for over an hour marching down a country road called Fleming Falls Road. By 2:30, the sun had taken its toll on the boys. Their shirts were soaked with sweat, and their pace had slowed to a crawl. Fleming Falls Road was a good choice from a safety standpoint. It was used almost entirely by farmers who gained access to it for transporting equipment from one field to the next and the occasional trip to town. Unfortunately, there wasn't much to see, because of the tall stalks of corn that bordered the road.

The boys were now passing the Gardner farm. Zoeller was leading when they came to a dip in the road. For the first time in over a mile, they could see over the corn. Robert saw something in the field only a few yards out. It was a large dark mass. He couldn't identify what it was, so he dropped out to investigate.

Clearly somebody or something had recently entered the cornfield at that spot. The stalks had been knocked down creating a path that led to the dark mass.

Robert followed the path until he came to a small clearing. He stopped and stared in disbelief at the heinous sight before him. His feet froze in horror. His hands began to shake; his knees ready to buckle. He suddenly felt his stomach rumble and before he knew it he watched in horror as the yellow muck of his breakfast and lunch splashed on the ground splattering his shoes and pants. He wanted to run out into the field, run as fast as he could and as far away as his lungs could endure. Nobody should have to see something like this, especially an eighteen-year-old.

As he stood there unable to move, another fear struck him. He could hear the laughter and the chatter of the young boys just a few feet away. They were loud and noisy. It sounded as if they followed him into the field. He turned and peered through the stalks. Thank God! They were still on the road, still marching innocently right by a display too ghastly to believe. They must not see this. It was too horrible for adult eyes, and would most certainly leave a scar if not totally alter the mind of boys as young as these.

Robert walked with nonchalance back to the road. He wanted to give the impression that what he found in the field was benign and really was a waste of time and effort. As he returned to the road, the boys paid him little or no heed. Reverend Veler, who was at the rear of the pack, noticed that there was something different about Robert. His face was ashen and without expression. Robert fell behind the Reverend.

"Are you okay?" asked Reverend Veler.

Robert motioned for him to stop while the boys marched on. "There are three dead bodies out there," whispered Robert, his voice shaking.

"What?"

"Out there, in the cornfield. It's horrible."

Veler peered into the field, unable at that angle to even see the mass that had attracted Robert.

"You have the boys stop at the top of that hill and wait for me," he said.

Veler walked over to the path and entered the field. It was as if the corn was alive and swallowed him as he entered their domain. His heart began to race; his hands shook. He hoped that Robert was wrong or was perpetrating some sophomoric joke on him. Yeah, that must surely be it. He will find some laughable prank in the clearing, return to the road and the sadistic laughter of sixty-five youngsters. Yet, there was something sinister about this path. It would have required a grown man, maybe two, to have knocked these six-foot stalks to the ground. Besides, Robert was much too responsible to have destroyed that much corn in the name of a prank.

Finally, Veler reached the clearing. He gazed in horror at the carnage in front of him. Never before had he seen such a sight. Three nude bodies lying on the ground drenched beyond recognition in their own dried blood. The ground and the stalks that surrounded the clearing were soaked as well. The fly-covered bodies were slightly bloated from the searing heat; the smell was already overwhelming.

Veler was stunned. He dropped to his knees and began to pray and cry at the same time. What should he do? He had never encountered anything like this before. The kids. He had to protect the kids. Now he understood what Robert had experienced. He needed to get the boys away from here and get to a telephone. Whatever happened here needed to be reported as quickly as possible.

Veler slowly got to his feet, his knees shaking uncontrollably. "Dear God, help me," he muttered and started back towards the road.

By the time he returned to the pack, they had grown impatient and were anxious to resume their hike. Veler and Zoeller exchanged knowing glances but said nothing. One of the boys asked what he had found in the field, and Veler replied as calmly as he could muster that there were dead hogs in the field.

Another quarter mile up the road was the Winger farm. Veler had the boys stop and rest on their front lawn that was nearly entirely shaded by a huge oak tree. While Robert kept the boys occupied, Veler went to the house and told Mrs. Winger what he had found. She called the sheriff, who, in turn, called the State Highway Patrol and the coroner's office. Already suspecting the identities of the bodies, Frank Robinson called the officials at the reformatory as well.

Within minutes, the area was swarming with cars and personnel. Fleming Falls Road was closed for a two-mile stretch, and deputies cordoned off the crime scene.

Robinson got out of his car and walked over to the entrance to the cornfield. There were two deputies standing guard.

"Don't let anybody in here except the coroner and the lab boys," said Frank to the guards. "I want this area sealed off while we search for evidence."

Boldly and without hesitation, Frank marched into the cornfield. He meant no disrespect for the dead. It was just that his mind was so preoccupied with details that he temporarily forgot what he was doing and what he was about to behold.

With a seemingly callous approach, he burst through the corn and into the clearing. His unwitting eyes fell on the scene. He gasped uncontrollably. Nothing in his years of experience as an officer of the law had prepared him for this. He paused, taking in the scene and trying as a well-trained professional to memorize the details. He knelt down beside one of the bodies. It was the only one that was a man. He never really knew John Niebel but had seen photos of him. There was no question in his mind that this was the remains of John Niebel, his wife and daughter. He examined the top of John's head and could clearly see an entrance wound. He glanced at the others and was reasonably certain that all three had been shot in the head. Evidence indicated that blood shot from the wound and splattered on the cornstalks, eventually subsiding and merely pumping out onto the ground until their hearts stopped. He jumped to his feet realizing this was big, possibly more than he could handle, and required the best and most well equipped investigators in the state. He hurried through the corn and got back to the road just as the crime lab boys arrived.

News of the tragic discovery spread across the country almost within the hour. It was the focus of nearly every headline in newspapers across the nation and had even spread to nearby countries. Obviously, the big question was who was responsible for such a heinous act. Everyone was certain that it was the work of Daniels and West, but despite all the attention that the crime scene was given by some of the state's best investigators, no evidence was found to positively link them with this crime. Still, the investigation continued with an unwavering assumption that Daniels and West were the perpetrators.

Excerpts from Coroner D. C. Lavender's report of the autopsy and all its gruesome details were soon published in newspapers across the country. He determined that John Niebel, his wife, Nolana, and their daughter, Phyllis were taken nude or in scanty summer night clothing from their home at about 2 a.m. Their unclothed bodies were found more than twelve hours later in a cornfield off Fleming Falls Road, two miles from U.S. 42 and about six miles from the home from which they were kidnapped.

Lavender said that Niebel had been shot through the top of his head, the bullet coming out near his nasal passage. There were also indications that he was struck with a blunt instrument, but the blow was not sufficient to cause death.

Phyllis Niebel was shot through the back of the head on the left side, the bullet lodging under her right eye. His preliminary findings when he examined the girl's body during the post mortem was that she had not been assaulted. Months later, he would testify in court that she was indeed assaulted, and an "unnatural sex act" was performed on her.

Mrs. Nolana Niebel was shot through the head with the bullet lodging in the facial bones. X-rays were taken at General Hospital to determine just where the bullet came to rest. There was evidence that Mrs. Niebel might have been left to die. Officials said there were indications the body had moved.

The grisly details of the report were the subject of every conversation throughout the state and particularly in the Mansfield area. Children were not allowed outside after dark, and even during the day they were confined to the uncertain safety of their own backyard. Every opening of every house was bolted and locked, and porch lights were left burning all night long. Few adults were able to sleep, and even some, armed with weapons, stood guard over their families. The terror spread to surrounding towns. The rumors were rampant that the killers would soon double back into the area seeking more of their bloodthirsty thrills. Vacation plans were put on hold, and evening activities were canceled. Panic ruled the area, and not one person scoffed calling it unwarranted hysteria.

Close friends of the Niebels continued to seek answers as to how the killers obtained entrance to the Niebel residence. By virtue of the fact that John was on the staff of the Ohio State Reformatory, the Niebels had always been extremely cautious about admitting people into the home, and, in fact, kept the doors locked nearly all the time. If someone knocked on the door in the evening, they were asked to identify who they were before the door was unlocked. Because of these extreme precautions, it was difficult to believe that the killers had gained entry without force.

George Allarding, Assistant Superintendent at the reformatory, denied that a present inmate at the prison could have committed the heinous act. About 250 inmates sleep outside the walls at the farm dormitory. A check is made every half hour throughout the night, and the checks made that night were without incident. He noted that it had to be an outside job since nobody could have got out long enough between checks.

Allarding also denied knowledge of a rumored clash between Niebel and an inmate on Tuesday. Any instance of force by an officer is always reported to him, and there was no report filed by John Niebel.

Family members, friends, and relatives both close and distant grieved over the loss. Hundreds of Mansfield citizens formed crowds around the Niebel residence to, in some small way, express their condolences.

Loyal Niebel was devastated. He probed his mind trying to think of any circumstances that could possibly have provided a motive for the cold-blooded killing of his parents and Phyllis. Dazed from the grief and shock, Loyal mechanically went ahead with funeral plans at the Jones Funeral Home where the funeral services were to be held on Friday, July 23rd. Unfortunately, a drove of reporters found him and begged him for an interview. He told them that it had to have been a deep feeling of revenge to account for such an action. Even a warped criminal mind wouldn't do something like that over the theft of a few trinkets. Besides, none of the jewelry was missing. Phyllis was still wearing her wristwatch, and his father had his Masonic ring when they were found. He didn't know if his mother still had her wedding band on her finger but presumed as much since none of the other things were taken.

Russell Niebel didn't learn of the death of his parents and sister until hours after the bodies were found. He left Mansfield in 1946 to attend the American Television School in Chicago. He was informed of the murders by Chicago Tribune reporters and hopped on a train bound for Mansfield.

Frank Robinson didn't sleep that first night. The image of the crime scene was painfully etched in his mind. It kept playing over and over in his mind. No matter what he did, it wouldn't stop. The bloated bodies, the blood, the shattered skulls where a chunk of lead had pierced them. Then there were all the facts, the evidence and leads, like tiny little puzzle pieces lying on a table waiting to be matched up and put together. All these things kept running through his brain. He rolled from one side of the bed to the other trying to fall asleep. He thanked God over and over for preventing those 65 kids from accidentally discovering the gruesome scene. For Frank, it was more example of God's gentle hand.

Frank couldn't stand it any longer. He got dressed and drove to the Niebel house. It was one o'clock in the morning almost 24 hours after the kidnapping and subsequent murders. The crowds had dispersed long before dark, and Frank had the house to himself. It was refreshingly a cool night. There was the threat of an approaching rainstorm, and it had fortunately ushered in a drop in the temperature.

Frank stood in the front lawn staring at the now empty house. The people who collected on the front lawn during the day meant well. Most came to pay their respects, but it all turned into a circus atmosphere. There were even vendors milling through the crowds selling food and drinks. It was quiet now, an almost eerie quiet. Even the crickets and all the other summer night noises were silent. It was if the world was in mourning…at least that part of the world.

Frank was still puzzled and a bit confused from the day's events. It had been a whirlwind of discoveries, phone calls, and speeches and no time to reflect on how all the puzzle pieces fit together. It was obvious that two men entered the Niebel residence at or around 1:30 in the morning. How they were able to persuade John Niebel to let them in is still a mystery that can only be answered now by the killers. They must have awakened the other members of the family and brought them downstairs. They must have been there for a considerable amount of time when one counts the number of cigarette butts found throughout the house. Because the house had been ransacked, it could be assumed that it was a robbery, and, yet, money and expensive jewelry were left behind. Since there were no signs of blood anywhere in the house, it could also be surmised that there was no resistance by John Niebel and no ill treatment by the intruders. For some reason, they were all down in the basement, then left the house through the back door. For some unknown reason, they drove them to a cornfield six miles away, had them take off their clothes and shot them in the head. The sequence of events was clearly understood. However, the motive remained a mystery. It was clearly not a robbery, and all evidence indicated it was not some random killings. It would seem that the killers knew the Niebels, and quite possibly they knew the killers. Even though they found no evidence at the crime scene linking the murders to Daniels and West, in his heart, Frank Robinson was convinced they were the right suspects.

Frank felt something else in his heart. He felt pain when he finally had time to think about the Niebels. Everyone who knew John and Nolana characterized them as wonderful people. What would they have discussed today? Probably retirement plans were a regular topic. They were planning a vacation, something they hadn't done in years. It wasn't because they couldn't afford it or that they didn't like to travel, it was simply because of

John's devotion to his job. Nolana hosted a group of women on a regular basis. They made quilts and canned vegetables to give to the needy. She probably would advise John when the next meeting would be held so that he could make plans to be elsewhere. Then, there was Phyllis. What a shame. What a Goddamn shame. What kind of monsters would cut down a young woman at the threshold of her life? So young, everything to live for. She had her life ahead of her. She'll never get married, never have kids. If ever I had a reason to catch these guys, it's for you, Phyllis.

It had been a tough day, all right. Lord knows Frank had earned his pay. It was now 1:30. He wondered what this new day would bring. Would this be the day they capture Daniels and West? He looked forward to an interrogation of the two men. If they were responsible for the Niebel murders, he would get them to confess. There was no doubt in his mind. All he wanted was the opportunity. Just give him an hour alone with those two. That's all. That's all he needed. If not a capture and confession, maybe he will finally discover the evidence that would positively link Daniels and West to the Niebel murders. Yes, sir, today ought to be a good one. The only scary thought is that maybe they're not done. Maybe the taste for blood has got a hold on them. They've already killed four people, and they can only electrocute you once. What's to stop them from killing again? Obviously, they have seen the papers and know that the entire state is after them. Instead of fleeing or going into hiding, they might kill again. It would almost seem as if they expect to get caught and might as well satisfy their lust for killing. Frank was convinced that this was the case. They were certain that eventually they would be killed for their deeds, so why not kill again?

Frank looked at his watch. It was going on two. "Good God," he muttered. He looked up at the house silhouetted in the moonlight. Twenty-four hours ago, an unspeakable horror was committed in the dwelling before his eyes. How he wished he could have been there. How he wished John had not answered the door. If only they had been on vacation. If only John had slept through the night without waking. If only. If only.

Frank took one last look at the house. It looked so sad. Its windows were eyes that stared back at him. He had one more if only. If only the house could talk.

Chapter Thirteen

In a small, dingy motel room on the south side of Cleveland, Robert Daniels and John West sat on the beds drinking cheap beer. Empty bottles were scattered about the floor, and a half-eaten sandwich had been smashed into the carpet.

It was late in the evening, and the boys had been drinking since they arrived in Cleveland nearly eighteen hours earlier. It was incredibly lucky that the young woman at the desk did not recognize them. By then, every early morning edition of every newspaper in the country had their pictures on the front page. Even though no evidence was found that positively linked the boys with the Niebel murders, the media still ran the story. To avoid the possibility of future litigation, they generously used the word "suspects." With the strong evidence and the eyewitness accounts that linked them with the Ambrose murder, they felt confident that they were safe by including the Niebel murders as well.

West drained the last drop from his bottle of beer and threw it across the room. It crashed against the plaster and lathe wall leaving a small hole and sending splinters and shards of glass flying across the room. He opened another and gulped from it.

"This beer is warm," said West. "We need to go find cold beer. Maybe we ought to go find a bar. I'm getting hungry."

"Are you crazy?" asked Daniels. "Everybody in America knows what we look like by now. We'd be spotted in a minute."

"Well, what are we going to do? We're going to have to leave this place sometime."

Daniels slurped his beer. "We're going to hold up here in this room until tomorrow night. Then, we'll leave under the cover of darkness."

"It's dark out right now. Why don't we leave town while we can?"

Daniels held out both arms spilling beer on the bed. "What's the matter with this place? Let's just rest up a bit."

"Where are we heading tomorrow?"

"We're heading west, young man. Gettin' the hell out of this state."

"Let's go now."

"No, I kinda like this place. Besides, maybe we can find some girls."

"I don't think so," muttered West.

"Why not?"

"You know why."

"No, I don't. Tell me."

"I'm ugly. That's why."

"Peggy didn't think so."

"Yes, she did."

"What are you talking about? She let you screw her."

"Don't forget. She thought I'd lost my mother. That was a mercy screw."

"What the hell makes the difference as long as you get laid?"

"I suppose you're right."

Daniels chugged his beer. "Don't forget. Women will fake an orgasm to get a relationship, and men will fake a relationship to get an orgasm."

West sprayed beer as he broke out in laughter.

"You know what would really be fun?" asked Daniels with an evil smile. "You're screwing some girl, and just as you finish, you pull out a gun and pop her in the head."

West snapped his beer from his lips. "That's sick."

Daniels formed a gun from his hand and pulled the trigger three times. "You didn't think it was sick when I popped those three in the cornfield."

"As a matter of fact, I almost threw up."

Daniels became angry. "Well, who the hell do you think you are? Don't forget, you're the one who dropped the hammer on that bar owner."

"That was different. That was self-defense."

"You killed him just the same," said Daniels smiling proudly as if he had scored a victory.

"That man was reaching for a shotgun. He would have splattered us all over that bar. Those three today weren't even armed. They were good people, hard working people. They didn't even know us let alone cause us harm. I worked for Mr. Niebel. He was a good man. He was tough. Didn't take no shit, but all the cons liked him 'cause he was fair. The talk was to keep an eye on the man since he had a bad heart. Never knew a convict that cared about a guard, before I met up with Niebel."

"Stop it. You're making me cry," said Daniels. He drained his beer and stumbled across the floor to get another one. "All I know is I had the experience of a lifetime."

"What experience is that?" asked West.

Daniels smiled. "Pullin' that trigger. Damn that was messy. I'd heard a head shot was messy, but I didn't know it was like that. I know it sound sick, but I swear I got a hard-on."

"How could you possibly get that excited from killing another human being?"

Daniels formed a gun from his hand again and pointed it at West. "It's the power thing. I hold the power of life and death in my hands. Nobody can tell me what to do. Nobody is laughing at me when I point that gun at his head. I have the power. I have the power over all things. I could have screwed Niebel's wife right in front of him, and he wouldn't have done a thing. I could have made him crawl around on the ground like a dog, and why? 'Cause I got the power. I could have let them live. Lord knows I probably should have spared the girl. She was so young and all. Such a pretty thing too. But if I had, she'd have fingered us for sure, not that the world is having a problem pinning those killings on us. All I know is that it was an exhilarating experience. More than likely, they're gonna fry me in the electric chair for it. Ain't no way we're gettin' away with this. They'll hunt us like dogs until they find us, but what a way to go. I tried to go straight. I tried to be like Dad. Hell, I tried to be like the Niebels. I couldn't even hold a job. Guys like us have only one destiny, and that's hell. We're going straight to hell. Might as well get it over with, so we don't hurt too many more of the good people. Wonder why God invented us in the first place. Of course, maybe He didn't. Maybe the devil invented us, since we're so evil. That's it. We're sons of Satan. That sounds pretty good, doesn't it? Maybe I should request that they put that on my tombstone. What do you think?

West grinned. "I think you're nuts."

Daniels rolled over on the bed. "You might be right. I know I'm drunk. That's for sure."

"Could have fooled me."

"Turn out the light. Let's get some sleep."

Chapter Fourteen

JULY 22, 1948: In spite of his lack of sleep, Frank Robinson was in his office at 8:00. The phones were already ringing, and there was a pile of notes on his desk from people who had already called. Within an hour, he had planned his day and was out the door.

Mrs. J. Paul Simpson was the first stop on his list. She lived north of town on State Route 13. Two strange men had come to her home Tuesday evening between 6:00 and 7:00 asking for gas. When she asked where their car was, they replied that it was "up on 13." She described the two men as young, in their 20's or 30's. One was average height, blond, with a ruddy complexion. The other was short and dark. Both were without hats or coats.

Mrs. Simpson told them that she had no gasoline and suggested the airport. The Simpson home was the last house on the left side of the road before reaching the airport.

Mrs. Simpson was a bit nervous since her husband was out of town at the time. The men left, but she did not believe they went to the airport.

Frank was satisfied that the two men she described were Daniels and West. It was good information and a good puzzle piece since it put them in a place at a certain time, but it didn't prove anything.

While Frank was in the neighborhood and had to drive right by the Niebel house, he decided to stop and look around now that he had a little more time. The crowds were already starting to form in the front yard, and the crime lab boys were busy at work. Frank excused himself and promised not to disturb anything.

He could see that there were subtle details that he had missed the day before. Details that meant nothing. Details that would be of little use in solving the crime or finding the criminals, but they were details that fascinated Frank all the same. They were common household objects one day and little memorials the next. On an end table next to the sofa, was a copy of *Pride and Prejudice* with a pair of ladies' reading glasses on top of it. It had a bookmark at page 167. Even if the reading glasses were not there by the book, Frank knew it belonged to Nolana. No respectable man would read a book so slanted towards women. Frank even knew what John would have had for supper. In the icebox were two large pork chops wrapped in white butcher's paper. He wondered what she had planned to serve with them. Mashed potatoes with gravy, and a vegetable sounded good. He closed the icebox and noticed an apple pie on the countertop, untouched and wrapped in wax paper. He even knew what was for dessert. Upstairs, on a nightstand beside a double bed, was a Bible with a silk bookmark saving the place in the Book of Mark for its reader. That was John's side of the bed. The deep impression in the mattress marked the weight and torso of a man, and the pillow on the other side of the bed had Nolana's long tresses of hair. Frank picked up the Bible and turned to the inside cover. "Happy birthday, John, 1908," was written in pencil. It was a birthday present on his tenth birthday. Too bad the giver didn't sign his name. Frank walked into Phyllis' bedroom. There was a strange feeling in the room, almost as if someone was there with him. He sat on the edge of the bed. The room had been ransacked just like all the others, but the intrusion and violation of this room seemed somehow different. It was if a young and beautiful woman had been violated and forced to do things against her will. The drawers were pulled out and their contents spilled onto the floor. Two cigarette butts had been crushed into the carpet. It was obvious that two monsters had invaded and violated the safe haven and private world of an innocent young girl. It just wasn't right. Men kill animals to survive. Men kill other men in war, but men just don't kill the sacred bloom of a spring flower.

Frank walked downstairs and sat on the couch. He looked around at all he could see. Other than the violent destruction left by the intruders, the house was pristine and a stellar example of a day in the life of an All-American family. They were hard working Americans who paid their taxes, went to church, and believed in the goodness of their fellowman. Unfortunately, their untimely and unprovoked demise not only ended the lives of three members of the Niebel family, but it ended a little piece of the American way of life.

Frank walked away from that house a little more knowledgeable and a whole lot sadder. He carried with him a snapshot of a family and the way they lived until a few hours ago. It was a quiet house. Not knowing the fate of its owners, it stood patient and hopeful, waiting for their return.

Frank walked away, more determined than ever to bring justice and sanity back to the small world of Mansfield, Ohio.

Chapter Fifteen

It was dusk and just dark enough for Daniels and West to pack up the car without being seen. They had spent the day drinking and taking short naps and were both in surly moods. Many of the conversations of the day turned into arguments, some near fights.

Their plan was to head west maybe as far as California. They just needed to find a place where they wouldn't be recognized. Their first destination was Indiana, and unfortunately their route was to take them through a small town called Tiffin, Ohio. The misfortune was not to befall Daniels and West; rather a young newly married couple on their way home from visiting family.

It was a little after 10:30 when Mr. and Mrs. Smith were returning to their home near Tiffin after visiting her parents, Mr. and Mrs. Strausbaugh. The foursome had spent the evening playing cards and eating ice cream. The Smiths were both tired. It had been a long day. Mr. Smith was traveling at the posted night speed 50 mph.

Daniels and West were traveling in the same direction on the same road and at a speed of just 60 mph. Their moods had not improved since they began their trip from Cleveland. In fact, it had deteriorated from bickering to near fistfights.

"You know what?" said Daniels. "We need to get our hands on a different car. This one has been described in every paper in the country."

"Well, then, let's just take one."

"Just like that?"

"Why not?" asked West.

"Some people frown on someone taking their vehicle."

West patted his gun. "Well, maybe we can correct that attitude problem."

"You seem a bit riled tonight," said Daniels.

"I need a drink."

"Jesus Christ, you can't be serious. That's all we've done today is drink."

"You sound more and more like my mother."

"How 'bout we stop bickering for a while and find a new car?"

West turned and looked out the window. "There, run that one off the road."

"What?"

"Act like you're a cop and run his ass off the road."

"You're kidding me."

"Just do it."

Daniels pulled alongside the car. West pointed at the shoulder of the road, but it was too dark for them to see. Daniels pulled slightly ahead of the other car and turned into his path nudging him over until he was in the ditch. Both cars continued for a few feet before coming to a complete stop.

West got out of the car and slowly walked to the driver's side window.

"Let me see your driver's license, please," he said.

Smith turned and looked at his wife. Fear was etched on his face. These men were posing as police and yet had no uniforms or any identification that would make him think they were officers of the law. Smith dug into his back pocket and removed his wallet. He pulled out his license and held it for a moment not knowing what to do.

West snatched at it, but Smith held on. "You can't have that," he said. West was enraged with anger. He pulled out his gun and without hesitation fired point blank into Smith's left temple. Blood spurted out the window nearly hitting West. Smith slumped forward onto the steering wheel, his life quickly ebbing out of him.

Enraged, Daniels thumped the steering wheel of their car. "That was a dirty, nasty thing to do," he said.

Mrs. Smith screamed hysterically. In total disbelief, she tried desperately to hold her husband, but it was obvious that his body was now lifeless. She then looked over at West who was still holding his gun, and realized the dangerous situation she was now in. She opened her door and started to run.

West pointed the gun at the fleeing woman and said, "Get back into the car, or we'll kill you too."

She stopped her flight, turned around and slowly returned to the car. West forced her into the backseat while Daniels maneuvered the Pontiac back onto the road. West was stone-faced as he watched her cry hysterically.

Once Daniels had the Pontiac back out on the road, both men got out of the separate cars. As West slowly walked towards Daniels, Mrs. Smith saw her split second opportunity to escape. She dashed from the car into the yard of the farmhouse of W.W. Martin, screaming all the way to his front door. As a last minute chore before going to bed, Martin was locking up the house when he heard Smith's screams. He opened the front door to let her in and looked up to see a light-colored Pontiac speed away.

"Why the hell did you go and shoot that man?" asked Daniels.

"He pissed me off."

"What?"

"He wouldn't give me his license."

"Could you blame him? Would you turn over your license to losers like us?"

"Why the big fuss?"

"For God's sakes, we're blazing a path that anybody could follow."

"Weren't you the one who said they can only hang you once?"

"I think I said electrocute, but I get your drift."

West peered out the window. "I hate to say it, but we still need a new car."

"Keep an eye out," said Daniels. "We need to dump this thing now."

They drove another ten miles on Route 53 until they came across a small roadside park. It was heavily wooded with dense foliage but had overhead lighting to mark its existence.

"Pull in there," said West.

"Why?"

"Sometimes people stop in these parks to get a few hours of sleep."

Daniels slowed the car and turned into the park. They followed the gravel drive until it came to a clearing with picnic tables and outhouses. At the end of the park was a truck designed to haul cars from one location to another. There were four Studebakers on the back of this one. Obviously, the driver was taking a load of cars to a dealership, grew tired and stopped for a rest. It was a fateful stop for him, one that would be his last.

Daniels turned off the car lights and parked about a 100 feet from the truck. They got out of the car, guns drawn, and walked slowly towards the vehicle. West came around on the driver's side and jerked open the door. He aimed his gun into the darkened cab. The driver was slumped over onto the seat. Startled, he jumped to attention.

"Get out of the truck," commanded West pointing his gun at the man's head.

He was a heavy-set man in his early forties. Rubbing his eyes, he slowly crawled out of the cab and onto the ground.

"Come with me," said West. He grabbed him by the shirt and led him into a patch of bushes.

The driver's name was Orville Taylor. He was from Niles, Michigan, married and the father of two. His whole body shook because he sensed what was about to happen. He could see it in West's eyes, in his deliberate actions, and by the intensity with which he held his gun.

West said nothing. He pulled on the man's shirt bending his head forward. He fired two bullets into Orville's brain killing him instantly. Orville dropped to the ground, shaking in a convulsive state, blood pouring out of his wounds.

West stepped back and, for a moment, stared at his victim. He then pocketed his weapon and returned to the truck and a waiting Daniels.

West was smiling. "They can only hang you once."

"Get in the truck," said Daniels. "Let's get out of here."

***

Sheriff Steinmetz just got into bed when the call came in. Bill Martin was frantic as he explained that Smith had been shot right there in his front yard. Steinmetz called his deputy, Grover Leopold, and instructed him to meet him at the Martin farm. Steinmetz knew how distraught Mrs. Smith would be, so he swung by her mother's home and brought her along with him to the Martin's place.

Steinmetz wasted no time. He led the grieving woman to his car and closed the door. He started for the driver's side when his deputy stopped him.

"I need your permission to try something," said Leopold.

"What do you want to do?"

"I want to drive around a bit. It's just a hunch, but I think I can find these guys."

Steinmetz was slightly shocked. He had never known Leopold to take such an initiative. "Sure, go ahead," he said. "Be careful. I'd bet the farm that this is the work of those two killers, Daniels and West."

"Don't worry. I'll be careful."

Leopold watched as Steinmetz drove away taking Mrs. Smith and her mother back to his office.

Grover Leopold had only been on the force for two years, and when he announced that he had a hunch as to the whereabouts of Daniels and West, it came as a shock and a surprise to his boss.

He slowly drove north of Route 53 hoping to find an abandoned car or anything that might help him find the killers. Within a few minutes, he came across the same roadside park where Orville Taylor had been gunned down. He drove slowly around the gravel driveway until he came upon a light-gray Pontiac. That was it. That was the car used by Daniels and West. His heart was pounding in his chest. What should he do? He only had two years of training, and nobody prepared him for something like this. Should he approach the car? Surely they had seen the lights of his car. There were two of them, and he was alone. If they overpowered him, they would most certainly get away. Leopold found a pay phone in the park and called for help. Within fifteen minutes, fifty men from Tiffin and Fremont's police departments and the sheriff's offices arrived on the scene.

The officers approached and surrounded a house about 75 feet from the abandoned Pontiac. As the men stationed themselves around the house, two men knocked on the front door. An older woman by the name of Mrs. Price opened the door. She advised the officers that she and her son and daughter-in-law heard two shots and the sound of a truck pulling away.

The officers began searching the thick brush for clues or anything that might help. It was only a few minutes later that one of the officers found the body of Orville Taylor.

For the first time since the nearly two week nightmare had begun, they had hardcore evidence. After searching the infamous light colored Pontiac belonging to the two killers, they found a Thursday edition of the Cleveland Plain Dealer revealing the details of the Niebel murders. Other items included a cigar box full of silver amounting to about $100 and a .25 caliber German Mauser pistol, both in the car's trunk. They also found packages of cigarettes of the same brand left by the Niebel killers, cigars, toothbrushes, candy bars, a bottle of soda pop, and two pairs of ladies' dress shoes, one brilliant red and the other dark green imitation alligator. The red shoes were later identified as belonging to Phyllis Niebel. Also discovered in the trunk were the clothes used by the killers in the Earl Ambrose killing in Columbus. Out of all the articles found in the abandoned car, the most damning and incrimination piece of evidence found was John Niebel's driver's license.

***

Once again, Daniels and West escaped the law, this time by only minutes. They drove up Route 53 for another few miles and then turned off onto a gravel road. They followed it for another two miles until they reached a small clearing where they pulled the truck over and stopped.

"What are we doing?" asked West.

"They're too hot on our trail. We got to hide out for the night, so they will lose the scent."

West settled back in his seat. "I could use a little sleep anyhow."

"Me too," said Daniels easing back as well.

"Think we're going to make it?"

"What do you mean?"

"You know what I mean," said West. "It's just a matter of time, and you know it."

"Yeah, I suppose you're right."

"They ain't taking me back to prison. I'll die first."

"My friend, for what we've done in the last couple weeks, I don't think they have any intentions of putting us back in prison. I think they have plans to put our asses in the hot seat."

"Rather die by a bullet," said West. "At least, I might take one of them with me."

Daniels paused. "Hell, this might be it for us. Who knows what's in store for us tomorrow."

"Do you really think so?"

"Well, I'm hoping we can make it to Indiana, but I'll bet half the state's cops are in this area by now."

There was a long silence as both men pondered their fate.

"Do you believe in God?" asked Daniels.

West sat up. "Hell, no," he declared. "What a crook 'O shit that is."

Another long silence.

"Why? Do you?" asked West.

"Yeah, I believe in God," said Daniels.

West laughed aloud. "I don't believe it. You go around robbing and killing, and you believe in God?"

"I didn't say I was a good person, I just said I believe there is a God."

"So you believe there's some big guy up there in the clouds making all this happen."

"When I was a kid, I remember being told that you had to have faith in God. I never really understood what that meant until a short time ago. I read an article by the smartest man in the world, Albert Einstein, and he said that our brains are limited. In other words, they're only designed to comprehend so much, and there are many things we simply will never understand. How does the universe keep expanding, and where is it expanding to? What triggers the heart to start pumping in an unborn infant? How does a human form from two liquids coming together? These are things that nobody understands, yet, we have to have faith that they happen. God limited our brains, because I guess He figured we only need enough smarts to get along here on earth. Einstein said something else I'll never forget, and this is actually what made me open my eyes. He said that you have to be a fool not to believe that thought went into all this. Think about the human body. It's the most complicated, well-designed machine ever invented. This body of yours didn't just happen. There was a lot of very careful thought went into the design. At your joints, there are tiny sacs containing a fluid that is far more slippery than anything man can make. Yet, somehow those sacs continue making the fluid and lubricate your joints. Hell, consider this. Your body was even designed with a social conscious. When you have to pee or take a dump, your body gives you a warning. It gives you just enough time to go some place private so you don't embarrass yourself by shitting down you legs. Atheists say that we just happened. They say we crawled out of the sea or some such shit that's wilder than believing in God. This world and everything in it was thought out and designed by some Supreme Being. Actually, I think he was having fun inventing all the animals. There are some really unusual ones out there. There are ones that are dangerous, ones that are pretty, and ones that provide us with food. No, my friend, there's nobody can convince me that this all just happened. It's too complex…too complex for the minds of mere mortals to comprehend. And the good news is if you really do believe in God, then you must acknowledge that He is capable of creating all this. And if He can do all this, then He's powerful enough to hear the prayer of even a four-year-old as she says her prayers at bedtime. Don't mean to preach, but when I see a newborn baby with a heart and organs, bones that developed inside her body, all her senses intact, feet to take her where she wants to go and fingers to make her journey easier, I have faith that this was all designed by one great being."

"Sorry," said West. "But I still think it's a load of crap."

Daniels smiled. "So, tell me. How do you think this all got started? How was man formed in the beginning?"

"Don't give a shit."

"Well, that keeps your life simple."

"So how 'bout, Mr. God man? Can you say a little prayer to get us out of this mess?"

"I don't think it would do any good."

"What do you think is going to happen to you when you die?" asked West.

"Going straight to hell. No question about it."

"Well, let me ask you this," said West. "If you believe in God and what He can do to you for leading a bad life, why did you turn out the way you did?'

Daniels' face sobered. "That's the one question I can't answer. Why do guys like us do the things we do? You and I are evil. We don't belong here. I sometimes think we were spawned by the devil himself. God likes a variety of people. There's no doubt about that, but I can't believe he would purposely build losers like you and me."

A long silence followed. West thought about protesting Daniels when he referred to him as a loser, but decided it wasn't worth it.

Both men drifted off to sleep.

Chapter Sixteen

JULY 23, 1948: It was about eight in the morning when West awoke screaming incoherently. Daniels jumped to attention.

"What the hell is wrong with you?" asked Daniels.

"I took a bullet," he said still shaking.

"What?"

"I just had a dream that someone shot me in the head."

"That ain't a dream, that's a premonition," said Daniels.

"It was so real."

"I'll bet anything you saw what's coming your way."

"I don't know, but I'll tell you one thing, that scared me to death.

"Makes you wonder if you see or feel anything."

West sat up in his seat. "I don't know, but I say we get out of here."

"Wait a minute," said Daniels. "Chances are they have road blocks set up. They're looking for two men. I say one of us should hide."

"You get up in one of those cars," said West. "I'll drive. I look more like that driver we killed than you do."

Daniels grabbed two pistols and a rifle. He climbed on the trailer, pulled up a canvas and got inside one of the cars. West turned the rig around and headed back to the road.

***

Sheriff Roy F. Shaffer was manning a roadblock just six miles east of the small town of Van Wert, Ohio at the intersection of State Route 637 and U.S. Route 224. He had seen many things in his time, but he had never experienced a roadblock for two such infamous killers as Daniels and West. Even though half of all law enforcement officers were in the area for the biggest manhunt in Ohio's history, personnel was stretched thin by the vast number of roadblocks set up in the area. In the past, any other roadblock would be manned by as many as six officers.

Traffic was light for a Friday morning, but then again it was only nine o'clock. Most of the approaching vehicles were driven by people recognizable to Shaffer and were allowed to pass through without challenge or inspection.

It was a little after nine when Shaffer first saw the car-hauler lumbering slowly towards him. Even though he could see that there was only one man in the cab, his highly developed senses as an officer of the law told him that something wasn't right.

Shaffer motioned for the driver to stop. He cautiously walked to the passenger's side of the truck and stuck his head through the open window.

"Morning," said Shaffer.

"Morning," said West.

"Anybody already stop you?"

"No," said West, his voice quivering.

"Anybody riding with you?"

"Not to my knowledge."

Shaffer stepped back from the truck. Conn was holding a machine gun and walked over to Shaffer.

"Something wrong?" asked Conn.

Shaffer pointed at West. "That driver is too nervous. Something ain't right."

"What do you want to do?"

"I'm going to get up there and take a look at those cars. You keep an eye on that driver."

Shaffer pulled himself up on the back of the truck. There were two decks of cars, two cars per deck. He climbed over to the first car and pulled back the canvas. He peered through the back glass. There on the back seat was a hat. Shaffer's heart raced. He knew that he had something. He ripped the canvas off the car. Shaffer peered into the side window of the car, and saw a man cowering on the front seat. He pointed his gun at the car.

"Get out of the car," said Shaffer.

The door slowly opened and Daniels slid out with his hands in the air. "Don't shoot. You got me. Don't shoot." Shaffer ordered him to get down off the truck.

Just as they both hit the ground on the passenger side of the truck, West opened the driver's door and jumped to the ground. He had an army rifle in his hands, shouldered it and began to fire. One bullet struck Frank Fremont in the arm, and he fell to the ground. Another hit Leonard Conn in the chest. As his knees crumpled and he began his fall to the ground, he opened fire with his machine gun. It was a short burst, but one of the bullets hit West between the eyes. West dropped to the ground, mortally wounded, with blood pouring from the wound in his head.

Within minutes, the area was swarming with police cars and ambulances. John Coulter West was taken to a hospital in Van Wert where he died at 11:18 a.m. Daniels was rushed to the county jail in Van Wert where he was locked up and put under heavy guard. Frank Fremont was lucky. The bullet that hit his arm pierced only the flesh and did no serious damage. He was treated and released a few days later. The bullet that hit Leonard Conn, however, was nearly fatal. At one point, the doctors had given up and were waiting for him to die, but he pulled through. In fact, his recovery was so extraordinary that he attended Daniels' trial just two months later.

So, ended the bloodiest crime spree in Ohio's history. Veteran police officers compared the Daniels-West pair with the Dillinger gang of the early 30's. There were those who called the Ohio Reformatory parolees "punks" by comparison with the Dillinger gang. There were others, and they included many officers who were in the thick of the hunt for both the Dillinger gang and the Daniels-West killers, said: "The Dillingers were Sunday school boys by comparison. Sure, they robbed and they plundered, but they never killed unless they were cornered. Daniels and West killed apparently for the sheer joy of killing."

There was a widespread sigh of relief as the news of Van Wert shootout spread across the nation. Children were once again allowed to play outside. Doors were still heavily locked at night but many were now left unlocked during the daylight hours.

In a blue-collar neighborhood on the south side of Columbus, Ohio, a reporter for the Columbus Dispatch newspaper stopped in front of a small, ivy-covered ranch home. He wrung his sweaty hands in nervous excitement. The location of this home had been kept a guarded secret until now. He walked to the porch and knocked on the front door of Mr. and Mrs. Daniels.

"Is my boy alive?" was the greeting he received as he walked through the front door.

The father sat silently across the room, his face grim and worn.

"I prayed so hard for my son not to be shot," she said. "I prayed day and night. We're glad he's alive, but they'll probably send him to the electric chair."

"I want it all to be a closed book," the father said. "We raised our boy right. We did the best we could. We're good people. If it hadn't been for Dillinger and the way they almost made a hero of him years ago when my son was young, maybe my son wouldn't be in trouble today. The time he spent in the Reformatory didn't help either."

In Mansfield, a reporter for the Mansfield News Journal interviewed Red Harris. He dismissed Daniels' assertion that they intended to slay Harris but killed three members of the Niebel family when they couldn't find Harris.

"I was at home in bed Tuesday night when the Niebels were kidnapped and killed," said Harris. "I don't know why Daniels didn't carry out his attempt if it was me he wanted to kill, nor do I know why he wanted to get me. I didn't know either Daniels or West."

Harris went on to say, "We all have our time to go. My time just hadn't come. That's all."

It was 3:00 in the afternoon of Friday, July 23rd, when the funeral proceedings began for John Niebel, Nolana Niebel, and Phyllis Niebel, just six hours after the shooting of John West and the incarceration of Robert Daniels.

Over 1,500 relatives, friends, church, lodge and business associates filed through the Jones Memorial the previous evening to pay their respects. Even though services at the Jones Memorial were designated as private, the funeral home was packed with over 300 people while hundreds stood on the porch or on the lawn discussing in muted voices the tragic events of the past three days.

Reverend Hagelbarger presided over the service. His talk was two fold in theme. He first spoke of the fine life that John, Nolana, and Phyllis had lived.

"I want to say words of appreciation for these Christian lives. They have been one of the finest families I have ever known down through the years. They were a happy family, kind and thoughtful, spreading goodwill among their many, many friends. They were not only members of the church but lived deeply its spiritual life, and their religion was real as demonstrated in their lives. They were choice personalities because their purpose in life was the highest."

For the second part of his speech, Reverend Hagelbarger spoke to the two sons, the brothers and sister. He took words of comfort from John 6:68.

"Lord to whom shall we go? Thou hast words of eternal life."

"We go in times of sorrow to the One who gave these eternal words, to the Father who cares about His children. Nothing can separate us from His love."

Reverend Hagelbarger went on to say, "You have the comfort of your many friends. And you have, too, the comfort of the Master who said, 'Come unto me, all ye that labor and are heavy laden and I will give you rest.' The eternal God, Himself, gives us comfort as real as that of a parent."

It was a somber occasion with bowed heads and quiet weeping. As the service came to a close, a parade of family and close friends slowly filed by the caskets in a display of deep respect and condolence.

Later that afternoon, the three members of the Niebel family were buried in Mansfield Cemetery. Nearly two thousand people populated the grounds. Dignitaries and politicians including the mayor and the Governor of Ohio were present. Since the graves were located on the side of a small hill, nearly everyone had a clear view of the proceedings.

After a few brief moments while everyone gathered around the three caskets, Reverend Hagelbarger said a few words to the crowd. He said, "We stand today with heavy hearts bowed down today with deep sorrow. This tragic event has been a severe threat to the decent living of city, community and all humanity." He, then, directed a private and personal message to the family and closed with a prayer. The proceedings were completed in less than ten minutes.

The throngs of people who had gone to so much bother just to attend glanced at each other in disbelief. They shuffled about, exchanged small talk, then slowly dispersed.

In Van Wert, a crowd was growing around the Van Wert County Jail where Daniels was being kept. It was an angry crowd close to becoming unruly. With Daniels' safety in mind, he was moved to a new, much stronger jail in Celina, Ohio. Daniels stood at the bars of his jail cell and said that if he ever got the chance he'd get Red Harris yet. Once again, he claimed that Harris "beat the hell" out him, and that he had planned for four years to get him. "If it wasn't for Red Harris, I wouldn't be in here now. I got a lot of Irish in me, and when somebody does something to me I get him back. If I ever meet Harris, I'll kill him."

Over the next few days, three counties were vying for the right to prosecute Robert Daniels. On July 29th, Common Pleas Judge Eugene Mc Neil of Van Wert County ordered Daniels to be released to Richland County officials for trial in Mansfield on a triple murder trial. It was believed that they had the best opportunity to put Daniels away so that he couldn't endanger anybody again.

Prosecuting Attorney Theodore Lutz and Sheriff Robinson arrived at the Mercer County Jail in Celina, Ohio to take custody of Robert Daniels. Frank Robinson was secretly excited and anxious to finally come face-to-face with this "Mad Dog Killer" as the local media had called him. He had been in pursuit of Daniels for what seemed like an eternity. It had occupied all his time, his thoughts, and his very life and could very well have been called an obsession by anyone who knew him.

Frank wasn't sure what to expect when he met Daniels. Someone had described him as "cocky and arrogant." He couldn't imagine someone in his predicament still maintaining such an attitude. In fact, he would expect, at least, a humble approach for someone in jail for murder, if not fright or even intimidation.

Robinson and Lutz entered the jail and met Sheriff Shaffer. They shook hands and exchanged small talk. After a few minutes, Lutz interrupted and reminded Robinson of the long trip ahead of them and the need to get started.

Shaffer took them through a door that led to the cells in the back of the building. Daniels was standing against the bars. His hands were shackled to a thick leather belt, and his feet were shackled together preventing him from walking at a normal pace.

Frank walked over to the cell. He was within a foot of the lean, blonde-haired man. He forced a grim, an almost triumphant grin.

"So, we finally meet," said Frank.

"You must be the winner of the spoils," said Daniels with a broad grin. "How lucky thou art."

"You had us going there for a while," said Frank.

Daniels' smile disappeared. He turned to Shaffer. "If I hadn't fallen asleep in that car, I wouldn't be here now, and you and that other guy would be dead right now."

"Hey, now, mind your manners. We have a trip to take, and we need to all get along," said Frank.

An arrogant smile returned to Daniels' face. It was if the anger he expressed left him as quickly as it came.

"I'm at a disadvantage here," said Daniels. "You, obviously, know me, but I don't have the same privilege."

Frank pointed at Lutz. "That man is Mr. Lutz. He is the prosecuting attorney back in Mansfield, and I am Sheriff Robinson."

"Oh, come on, now," said Daniels. "We're all going to be together for quite a while. Can't we relax a little and go by first names?"

Frank smiled in defiance. "That man is Mr. Lutz, and my name is Sheriff Robinson."

"And here I thought we were going to become good friends, even drinking buddies," said Daniels.

Lutz cleared his throat. "Let's go, Frank."

"Did I hear him say Frank? I knew we'd be on a first name basis."

Shaffer rattled a giant key in a hole in the door and swung the door open.

"Yes, let's get going on our long trip," said Daniels. "We can chat and catch up on old times."

Inside, Frank was appalled at the brazed attitude and the total disregard for what he had done or the seriousness of the situation. He was angered but knew he didn't dare show it. The last thing he wanted to do was to alienate the man. He needed to create an easy atmosphere; one that Daniels would feel comfortable enough to talk freely. Besides, he didn't want to give Daniels the satisfaction of knowing he had "got" to him.

Robinson and Lutz had brought an unmarked police car to avoid as much attention as possible. It was a black car just a few years old and had a caged backseat. Lutz drove, and Frank got in the backseat with Daniels. It was not a normal arrangement for an officer to be locked up with such a notorious and hardened criminal, but Frank thought that Daniels might be more relaxed without looking through bars. Surprisingly, Sheriff Shaffer rode in the front seat with Lutz. Normally, when a criminal has been remanded to the custody of another officer, his responsibility has been completed, and yet Shaffer opted to assist.

"I suspect I have a date with old Sparky, don't I?" asked Daniels. "Or is that disrespectful to be on such informal terms with such a formal, or should I say formidable, device known as the electric chair?"

"You'll get a fair trial in court," said Frank.

"Let's cut the crap, Frank. I'm tomorrow's burnt toast, and you know it. But that's okay. I have it coming to me. I did it. You'll get no argument from me on that. In fact, I'll make a confession right here and now. I know that's what you're waiting to hear. I know that's why you're being so nice and even sitting back here with a known killer. I did it. I killed all three of the Niebels. Johnnie killed the others, but I want credit for the Niebels. I popped 'em right in the head with my Mauser. Had to have hurt, don't you think? Maybe, not. The old man dropped like a sack of potatoes. I think he was dead before he hit the ground. One of the women, I don't remember which; I think it was the girl, was still moving after taking one in the melon. Imagine that. I actually felt bad about shooting her. She was young...way too young. Her folks were old and gonna die someday anyhow. I just hurried them along a bit."

By that time, Frank was in shock at what he was hearing, but he kept his emotions in tact. "Tell me about West."

"Johnnie? Johnnie was a good friend. Met him in prison, you know. Good kid, but dumber than shit. His I.Q. was only 60. I think that's somewhere between a rock and a bucket of snot. But we got along really well. Guess that's because we were both losers. Big time losers. All our lives kind of losers. I've often wondered why God invents people like Johnnie and me. Seems like such a waste of his time and effort. I think he puts us on earth to serve as an example of a low life. It gives people a positive sense of self-worth. Makes them feel good about themselves, you know?"

"My goodness, Mr. Daniels..."

"Call me Robert. There's no need for formality under the circumstances."

"Alright. I'm surprised at what you said. It almost sounded like you might believe in God."

"Oh, I most certainly do."

"That's incredible."

"Why? Because I killed someone?"

"Well, it would seem that..."

"Someone can believe in God and still commit a sin, even if it's in the top ten of sins. I've said this many times, Frank. You have to be a fool to not believe that thought went into all this. Know who said that?"

"Well, not really."

"Albert Einstein, the smartest man who ever lived. He said that. You gotta admit, Frank, he makes a lot of sense. Someone once said that there's no such thing as a coincidence. I sure hope that when you guys stopped us and I was asleep at the time, that was a coincidence, 'cause if it wasn't that means that God set us up. I don't know why I should care. I know I've pissed off God more than once, and He's got a special place for the likes of me."

"Do you think you're going to hell?"

Daniels laughed. "I can almost bet you he's already started a fire for my ass."

"You could still ask for forgiveness."

"I don't figure He works that way. I figure He don't answer any prayers until He's good and cooled down. After what I did, He ain't cooling off for a long while."

"You could…"

"Let's change the subject. I don't want to talk about God and stuff."

"Okay, Mr. Daniels. Why don't you tell me about your life of crime?"

"Oh, you want to hear the juicy stuff. Is that it? I'm surprised at you, Frank. That's a bad case of voyeurism, you got there. Well, can't say as I blame you. Maybe that's a positive service I provide for society. Maybe I provide shocking stuff for decent people to behold. I give their world order and sanity when they compare it with the chaos of mine. Well, let's see. My life of crime by Robert Daniels. I guess I got my start stealing cars if you don't count the petty stuff in school like stealing money from other kids. If you want to go back that far, you'd probably find that I started stealing when I was in diapers. Makes you wonder if I was born to be bad. When you find yourself tearing wings off flies and you're only two years old, you might be somewhat troubled. Anyway, I got thrown in the can a couple times for robbery, escaped once, and finally got paroled. Didn't much like it in there. You've got to be a fool to continue down a road of crime after being in one of those places. Inmates didn't bother me much. I think they were afraid of me. They thought I was crazy. Imagine that. Met up with Johnnie at Mansfield. That was probably the only good thing that ever happened in that place. He was an ugly bastard. Damn! He should have shaved his butt and walked backwards. And stupid too. God sure had it in for him. He didn't have a chance. It's best they put him out of his misery."

"Tell me, Mr. Daniels," said Frank. "How were you treated in Mansfield?"

The forever, arrogant smile left his face. His face went cold. "I can't believe we didn't go back and get Harris when we had the chance. That son-of-a-bitch made our lives a living hell. He used to hit us in the stomach, that way it didn't show any bruises. I missed my chance. If I ever see the light of day again, I'll get that man."

"How did you and West get started?"

"We had made a pact inside that we would get together after we were both out and get Harris. We needed some money, so we robbed a couple filling stations. Can't make much money doing those places. If you're going to risk going to jail, it might as well be over big money, so we decided to knock over a bar. The first one went pretty well, but the second one went bad. We netted $800, but we had to pop that Ambrose guy. What an idiot. Johnnie is holding a gun on him, and he thinks he can reach down under the bar and pull out a shotgun, aim and pull the trigger before Johnnie can squeeze his finger. How stupid can you get? He deserved to die. Man, that was a mess. It was just a handgun, but it looked as if it took his head clean off. It just kinda exploded. Blood and shit flew everywhere. Hell, when I shot the Niebels pointblank, it wasn't that bad. Oh, blood spurted like a fountain, but it only left a tiny hole. It's funny, but I swear I saw the bullet enter the old man's head. I don't suppose that's possible as fast as that thing is going."

"Tell me about the Niebels. The whole world would like to know why."

"After we killed that Ambrose guy, the heat was on. Jesus, you'd thought we'd shot the president. We were on the run and were in Michigan at the time. We decided to make a quick trip to Mansfield and settle up with Harris. Problem was we didn't know where he lived. I knew Niebel would know, and I knew where he lived. I'm really surprised he let us in that night. Two strangers knocking on your door in the middle of the night. We had some lame story about our car being broke down and he let us in to use the phone. What a mistake. What a big mistake. He went for the phone and I told him it was a stick up. Johnnie and I both had our guns out at that point. I had Johnnie keep an eye on Niebel while I went upstairs to see who was up there. I found the old lady and the girl. Scared them half to death. Johnnie told me later that he laid a handgun on the kitchen table and told Niebel to go for it. The big dummy should have tried. Anyway, we asked him where Harris lived, and he said the next house up the road. We needed time to deal with Harris, so we asked if they had any rope. Nobody in that Goddamn house could find any rope. We even went down in the basement, still no rope. You know, I've thought about that night a million times since it happened, and I can't believe that nobody thought about the clothesline in the backyard. We could have used that, and the Niebels would be alive today."

"What happened then?"

"We decided to dump them off in a field far away. That would give us time to deal with Harris. We took a wrong turn somewhere and ended up downtown. We drove around that square and headed back out of town. I don't remember the name of the road, but it took us out in the country right past the prison. What a surprise that was. Wasn't expecting to see that place again. We turned off on some back road that went right out in the cornfields. After a mile or so, we stopped, and everybody got out of the car. We led them back into the fields a few feet and stopped. Johnnie mashed a few of the cornstalks down, so we could have a little room. He had a hell of a time. Those stalks looked to be about ten feet tall. Suddenly, Johnnie tells them to take off their clothes. Damn, was I shocked. He had a grin on his face, so I knew what he wanted. He just wanted to see that girl. That's all. Not that I blamed him. She sure was a looker. Besides, it sounded like a good idea. Might slow them up on running for help. You know, I've often regretted doing that. Man should have a little dignity when he dies, don't you think? Even with the fear they must have been feeling, it had to have been humiliating for him to be standing there in front of his daughter like that. Actually, the whole scene was kinda pitiful, if you know what I mean. Sure was a waste, shooting that pretty young thing. Goddamn waste. Like I said before, we only took them out there to dump them off. Had no intentions of killing them. Then, something came over me. Can't really explain it. Tried to figure it out since it happened. I always wanted to do it, and this was the perfect opportunity. Done a lot of bad things in my life, but I never thought I would kill someone. Guess I always knew in the back of my head that it would eventually come to it. I told the old man he had two minutes to get right with God."

"Did anybody say anything?"

"The girl said something about it wasn't her dad's fault that he worked for the state."

"Is that when you shot them?"

"Shot 'em all in the head. The old man was first, the girl next, and the mother last."

Frank was now in shock. "Can't imagine the horror Mrs. Niebel must have felt," he muttered.

"Yeah, suppose you're right," said Daniels. "Never thought about it."

"You never thought about it!" said Frank with an angered voice. "How could it not bother you with your every waking minute? How could the terror in her face not haunt you?"

"Hold on there, Frankie. Don't forget I'm the villain with no conscious. If I had a conscious, I wouldn't have done it in the first place."

Frank paused as he collected himself. "Sorry."

"Now, let's see. Where was I? Oh, yeah. After that, we hightailed it out of town and held up in Cleveland for a spell. Then, we decided to head west. That's when we met up with that farmer over in Tiffin. The guy went and pissed off Johnnie. Man, was he mad."

"What happened?"

Johnnie was acting like a cop or something. Asked him for his driver's license, and when Johnnie went to take it, the guy said something about he couldn't have it. Lord, he signed his death warrant right then and there. I knew what Johnnie was going to do long before he pulled out his gun. Shot that guy right in the head right there in front of his wife. Damn, that was nasty, and I told him so. No need to do something like that. I think Johnnie was just trying to catch up with me on the body count. It seemed to bother him that I had more kills. Talked about it all the time. Ain't that a bit sick when you think about it? Anyways, we decided it was time to get a new vehicle. That Pontiac had been in every paper in the country. We drove on up the road until we came to a park. You know how some people pull in those places to sleep. Well, there it was, one of those car-hauler trucks. We rousted the driver out of his sleep and made him get out of the truck. From the way, Johnnie was acting, I knew what he was going to do. He grabbed the guy by the shirt and pulled him over into the weeds. He then pulled down on his shirt making his head bend forward. I felt kinda sorry for him at that point. Then, Johnnie shot him in the head. He dropped straight to the ground just a twitchin' like crazy. At that point, the whole thing seemed just like a nightmare that wouldn't quit. I couldn't help but think how could two people do things like that to another human being? I guess Johnnie got what was coming to him, and I'll get mine."

"What about the roadblock in Van Wert?"

"I guess every criminal sooner or later makes a mistake. If I hadn't fallen asleep in that car, I'd have killed those cops, and that's a fact."

"I'm surprised you didn't try shooting them anyhow."

"He had the drop on me. Never had a chance. He was pointing his gun at my head, and my weapons were too far out of reach."

"Ever have any regrets?"

Daniels leaned back and took a deep breath. For a moment, the arrogance and haughty attitude washed away from his face. He hung his head with a sober almost sorrowful look. "Yeah, I have regrets. I wish I'd paid more attention in school. Maybe I could have gone to college and got a good job. Never could hold onto a job of any sorts. Don't know why other than I didn't like taking shit from a boss." He paused for a moment. If I had it to do over, I wouldn't have shot that Niebel girl. That was a mistake. "Sorry about what my parents must be going through.

They don't deserve this. I'm not sorry I'm such an evil man. I don't think that was my doings."

"Whose fault is it, then?"

"God is the one who made me. I had nothing to do with it."

"So you think it's God's fault you killed the Niebels?"

"You didn't think someone like me would take the blame, did you?"

"You said something about a date with old Sparky. Are you afraid to die?"

Daniels paused for a moment. "Naw. Gotta expect to pay the price."

"Where do you think your friend West is right now?"

"He's dead, as in eyes closed, never to scratch his ass again."

"I mean do you think he went to heaven?"

"I knew what you meant."

"Well, what's your answer?"

"He's dead, simple as that. There ain't no heaven or hell, just death."

"I thought you said you believed in God."

"I do, but I don't think there's a heaven or hell. I can believe in God and not in the hereafter."

Frank smiled and leaned forward. "You know, I once heard it said that it's better to believe in God and find out there isn't any than to not believe in God and find out that there is a God."

"Very profound," said Daniels. "But don't you find that a bit hypocritical? Seems like a shallow reason to believe in God. You believe in Him to protect your soul not out of a true love and respect for the Creator."

"Good point, but who wants to risk eternal damnation?"

Daniels turned to Frank with an uncharacteristically sober face. "One point for Frank Robinson."

Nothing much was said for the rest of the trip, only small talk and idle chatter. Daniels dozed in and out of sleep; Frank sat quietly in deep thought.

Despite an order of Judge Eugene Mc Neill of Van Wert that Daniels should be confined in the Mansfield Reformatory for safekeeping, the accused slayer was taken to the county jail. Frank said it was because Daniels was in county custody until he is sentenced.

It was about 5:30 when they arrived at the jail. In his customary manner, Daniels swaggered down the sidewalk, posing readily for photographers. He did, however, mention that he would rather tidy up a bit before having his picture taken.

"Wait 'till I get my shirt collar straight," he said. "Maybe it would be better if I posed with a gun in my hand." Faces turned grim. Many of the photographers lowered their cameras but, eventually, snapped the pictures out of a sense of duty.

Incredibly, Sheriff Shaffer had developed a certain bond with Daniels. As Shaffer began to leave, Daniels told him: "Well, so long, buddy. I'll be seeing you." Shaffer reached through the bars of his cell and shook hands with him. He turned to the photographers and asked if they wanted a picture of them saying goodbye.

Daniels was held in the women's section of the jail under twenty-four hour guard. He was lodged in the corridor part of the women's section, since there is no one else in that part of the jail.

Robert Daniels was bound to the Richland County grand jury without bond on three counts of first-degree murder. On Friday, July 30th, he appeared before Judge H.H. Schettler a few minutes after 11 a.m.

"You are charged with murder in the first degree on three counts. How do you plead?" asked the judge.

Daniels sat straight in his chair. "Guilty," he announced in a bold almost proud voice.

The judge then began reading the murder charges first repeating the name of Nolana Niebel.

"I didn't know their names," muttered Daniels. "I just knew there were three of them."

As Daniels sat in the courtroom, his eyes wandered over the approximately 25 spectators in the room. He smirked in defiance with a total disregard for the seriousness of the moment.

Court proceedings were concluded in just two hours, and Daniels was returned to his cell. It was later in the afternoon, when Prosecutor Lutz and two deputy sheriffs showed up at Daniels' cell. They led him down the back stairs and out the back door to a waiting, unmarked police car.

"Where are we going, Mr. Prosecutor?" he said.

"Going for a ride," was his sharp reply.

The car sped off towards the downtown square and out of town on Route 13. They turned on Main Street Road, traveled less than a block and turned into the driveway of the Niebel house.

"What are we doing here?" asked Daniels staring at the empty house.

"Recognize this place?" asked Lutz.

"Of course, I do."

"Care to tell us anything about it?"

Daniels paused then smiled. "Owners should have invested in a little more rope."

Lutz turned in his seat. He stared at Daniels with an enraged glare. He said nothing and soon turned back around.

"Let's go inside," he said getting out of the car. They led Daniels, with hands and feet still manacled, to the kitchen. It was still in disarray with dishes and utensils spilled all over the floor.

"Mind telling us what happened that night?"

Daniels seemed unaffected, still swaggering with arrogance in the midst of the aftermath of a tragic event.

"It happened just like I told you before," said Daniels.

"Why don't you look around. Maybe something will jar your memory."

The two deputies led him into the living room. Daniels poked through things on the coffee table. He picked up a pair of glasses obviously belonging to either Nolana or Phyllis. He held them up to the light and smiled. "Someone had ought to clean these."

Lutz snatched them out of his hand. His hands quivered with rage. "I'd rather you not touch anything," he said.

Daniels turned to Lutz. "I'm impressed at your self-control. You're not showing it, but I know, right now, you'd love to break my neck. Am I right?"

Lutz said nothing.

"Come on, Lutz. It's just you and me and these goons. Get it off your chest and tell me what you think."

"Okay, Daniels," said Lutz. "I'll tell you what I think. I think you're a Goddamn coward."

"A coward? How could you call me a…"

"You shot an unarmed, defenseless man. Then, you shoot two women for God's sakes, and one of them was at the threshold of her adult life. Only a Goddamn coward would do such a thing. You're lower than snake shit and you deserve to die. The Niebels were a part of the backbone of this country. They're the glue that holds everything together. Scum like you doesn't deserve to live in this country. And your callous attitude about the whole thing is absolutely an abomination. I'd love to take that flippant tongue of yours and cut it out of your head."

Daniels gave Lutz a cold stare. "You're in trouble now. That was a threat," he said coldly. He turned to the two deputies. "Hey, did you two hear that?"

Without turning around, one of them said, "Hear what?"

Lutz gave Daniels a triumphant smile, and Daniels slowly turned away. For the first time since he had been captured, he was angry. He knew it was his word against the others. He stared at some pictures on the wall and walked over to the bed. On the nightstand was a Bible, and serving as a marker was a piece of paper. He pulled it out and stared at it.

"Damn it, Daniels, will you leave stuff alone?" asked Lutz.

"Phyllis was about to have a birthday," said Daniels.

"What?"

"This is a to-do list for her birthday coming up in a week. She was going to be twenty-one."

"Put it down, Daniels," said Lutz.

"She has to bake a cake, buy something for her hope chest, call friends and family. Somebody by the name of Carol Robinson is coming over to help."

Lutz snatched the paper from his hands. "Keep your filthy hands off everything in this house. "Come on guys. Let's get back in the car. This is going nowhere."

They climbed back into the car and started for town. They, then, turned onto another route that headed back out of town. It was then that Daniels knew where they were going. They turned down Fleming Falls Road and stopped after nearly a mile.

"Why are we stopping here?" asked Daniels.

"Recognize this place?"

"You know I do."

Lutz opened the car door. "Let's go take a closer look."

The clearing where the murders had taken place had been cleaned to a certain extent. Blood-soaked cornstalks had been removed and burned. The blood-covered ground had been, carelessly, turned over with a shovel leaving behind traces of red.

"Show me where they stood when you shot them," said Lutz.

For the first time, Daniels seemed nervous. He fidgeted with his fingers and lightly pranced about.

"What's the point?" he asked.

"I want to know."

"Is this a bad case of voyeurism?"

Lutz said nothing.

"Alright. I lined them up right over here," said Daniels pointing his finger.

"Why did you have them take off their clothes?"

"Humiliation can sometimes work in your favor. We figured that they would be that much more reluctant to leave the field."

"You wanted to see the girl without any clothes, didn't you?"

"No, that wasn't the reason."

"You raped her, didn't you?"

"Neither one of us touched her."

"The coroner says you did and is going to testify in court."

"He's lying."

"The doctor is going to back up his testimony."

"I swear I didn't touch her. Why would I lie? After all, I'm going to the chair for killing her."

Lutz paused for a moment as he calmed his enraged temper. He thrust his hand in his pocket and pulled out a heart-shaped locket on a chain. "Here," he said handing it to Daniels. "Did you ever see this before?"

"No. Why?"

"It belonged to Phyllis. It was found here on the ground."

"Never saw it before."

"Open it up."

"What?"

"Open the locket."

Daniels snapped the tiny locket open. On one side was a picture of Phyllis and on the other side was a picture of her boyfriend, Raymond.

"Who's that?" asked Daniels.

"You don't recognize the girl?" asked Lutz.

"Of course, I do."

"Tell me who she is, damn it. I want to hear you say it."

"Okay, she's the girl I shot. There, are you happy?"

"In case you might be interested, the guy is who she was probably going to marry, have kids with and live to a ripe old age. Of course, none of that will happen now."

Daniels stared at the open locket. His face was expressionless. It was if he was mesmerized. All at once, he snapped it shut and handed it back to Lutz. "I'm sorry," he muttered and slowly followed the others back to the car.

Chapter Seventeen

It was 10:00 a.m. on August 2nd when Daniels appeared before the grand jury. Crowds formed at both the courthouse and jail all hoping to get a glimpse of Daniels. As he got out of the car, he smiled at the girls waiting to see him. He was chewing gum and strutting as much as his shackles would permit.

Inside the courtroom was packed with as many onlookers as was permitted. Sheriff Roy Shaffer of Van Wert County made an appearance as did Sheriff Frank Robinson and the coroner D. C. Lavender of Richland County.

In one of the shortest sessions in years, the grand jury returned an indictment of three counts of first degree murder against Robert Murl Daniels. Obviously, it came as no surprise, and was met with little fanfare and even less concern.

Judge Kalbfleisch asked the defendant to approach the bench. Daniels walked to the front of the courtroom and stopped in front of the judge. Kalbfleisch pushed the microphone to one side and leaned over as far as possible. "We are concerned that you get a fair trial and that due processes of the law are observed. You have been indicted on charges of first degree murder on three counts. The charge is serious; one in which you may be acquitted or convicted and given the extreme penalty. Do you have an attorney?"

Daniels told the court that he was unable to employ an attorney, so Judge Kalbfleisch said he would appoint counsel by selecting one from the Richland County attorneys.

It was late the next morning that Lydon H. Beam got the call. He was officially appointed by the court to defend Robert Murl Daniels for three counts of murder in the first degree. He resented the appointment and spoke freely with Judge Kalbfleisch of his dissatisfaction if not annoyance with the decision. After serving the court for over twenty years, it was his contention that he deserved a certain level of respect and not be forced to defend a man who was, by his own admission, guilty of the crime. After all, he had his good record and prestige to consider. Of course, the national attention he would certainly get from this high profile case could possibly work in his favor. Beam considered both sides and finally out of pure frustration dismissed the debate going on in his mind. After all, he had no choice in the matter.

With two guards acting as an escort, Beam climbed the stairs of the county jail to the second floor. The floor was empty except for one cell where Daniels lay sleeping. One of the guards gently tapped on the bars with his nightstick rousing him from his sleep. He rubbed his eyes and squinted at his guests. He then unlocked the door to his cell and allowed Beam to enter.

"Mr. Daniels, my name is Lydon Beam. I'm your court appointed attorney."

Daniels sat up on the edge of the bed. "Who did you piss off?"

"Excuse me?"

"You obviously must be on somebody's shit list."

Beam dragged a wooden chair over to the bed in front of Daniels. "I still don't understand."

"You're going to chalk this one up for a loss. That's a given."

"Why, Mr. Daniels, you're already accepting defeat?"

"I don't know whether you've read the papers lately, but I confessed already. I was even so bold as to ask for the credit to the Niebel murders."

"Yes, that was a brazen if not fatal mistake on your part. Such arrogance was quite possibly more detrimental than the act of murder itself."

"I don't understand," said Daniels. "I already confessed. How much more guilty can I be?"

Beam closed his notebook and leaned forward. "There are different types of killings, and the public reacts differently to each. Obviously, a killing that is the results of one defending oneself is perfectly acceptable and is met with approval if not adulation and praise in some cases depending on the identity of the aggressor. Other killings are called murders of passion and usually are the results of relationships that have gone awry such as the ever-dangerous scenario of a man getting caught in bed with another man's wife. Such murders are met with, at the very least, raised eyebrows by some, condemnation by others. Then there are murders that occur, and the perpetrator arrogantly flouts society and the laws that regulate and maintain order.

These individuals are regarded by just about every facet of society as monsters and should be put to death without fail and with dispatch. Mr. Daniels, I'm afraid you have, precariously, put yourself into the latter category and have narrowed if not eliminated the odds of your getting a life sentence rather than the electric chair."

Daniels thought for a moment and then smiled. "My trial is not going to be heard by a jury," he said. "It will be a panel of three judges."

Beam leaned back with a smug look. "Mr. Daniels, don't be naïve. "These three judges have a duty and responsibility to, not only impose justice, but to represent the public's wishes, and in some cases, demands. Besides all that, they have feelings too, and when they encounter someone who has a total disregard for the law, it makes them a bit testy."

Daniels forced a grin. "So what you're saying is I'm a dead man."

"We have one and only one option left," said Beam.

Daniels sat straight. "What would that be?"

"Not guilty by reason of insanity."

Daniels pondered the idea. "So what you're saying is that I was crazy at the time."

"Exactly."

"Well, if it will help, I fell on my head when I was a kid."

Beam started to laugh at what he thought was humor, then his smile faded when he realized that Daniels was serious. "You fell on your head?" he asked out of disbelief.

"Two different times. Was unconscious for days."

Beam jotted down a note. "We might just have something here."

Daniels leaned back and beamed a proud smile as if he had accomplished a great feat.

Beam set his notebook and pen on the floor beside him and crossed his legs. "Now, Mr. Daniels, we'll get into the details when I have more time on my next visit. Right now, I want to ask you something and this is just between you and me."

"Ask away," said Daniels still smiling.

"There's no question but what you committed the crimes," said Beam. "That's been well documented. Mind you now, you don't have to answer this question, but I just want to know why. Why did you kill all those people?"

Daniels stared at Beam trying to decide if he would answer the question, and if he did, what he would say. He then folded his arms over his chest and leaned back in a defiant sort of posture.

"Why do you want to know, Mr. Beam?" he asked with a smug voice. "Sounds like you have more than a passing interest in such morbidity."

Beam said nothing, and Daniels considered his silence as a confirmation of what he had suggested.

"The bar owner asked for it," said Daniels in a glib, matter-of-fact manner. "He was reaching for a shotgun when Johnnie shot him. At that point, it was him or us. Hell, you're a lawyer. You could darn near call that self-defense, couldn't you?"

Daniels paused, waiting for a response. Beam was fidgeting with his hands and not even looking in his direction.

"It wasn't as if we were in there looking to kill someone. Far from it. We just needed a little cash. If that Ambrose guy hadn't been so greedy, he might be alive today.

"That farmer guy was another story. He wasn't doing anything wrong. He just didn't know Johnnie and his temper. The man ups and refused to give Johnnie his driver's license. I knew that man was in trouble. I could see it coming. You see the way it happened was Johnnie walked right up to the car on the driver's side. He strutted up there like he was some kind of cop and asked for the man's driver's license. He pulled it out of his wallet but for some reason refused to turn it over. Johnnie had such a wicked temper. He backed away from the truck shaking his head. I knew he was mad, but I didn't think he would do something like that. Afterwards, I told him so. I told him that was nasty and that there was no call for that. Anyways, he pulled out his gun and shot that poor man right in the head. My God, blood flew everywhere. It even splattered the missus. If the truth were known, we should have popped that pretty young wife of his. Next thing we knew she was running up to a farmhouse screaming and carrying on. I'm sure that didn't help matters much. Just one more witness and one more nail in our coffins. In a way, I'm not sorry she got away, such a pretty thing, innocent and all.

"It was about that time, we realize we need to get another vehicle. Hell, that Pontiac we had was mentioned in every newspaper in the country. We drove on up the road 'til we came to a park of some sorts. We figured that late of night, there had to be someone pulled over getting some sleep. Sure enough, there was a car hauler parked there. I was always surprised a big guy like that driver didn't put up a fight. Johnnie simply led him into the weeds and shot him in the head. So, I guess you could say we shot him because we needed his truck. All three shootings were for good reasons, but I have to say, I think Johnnie did it because he wanted to. I think he got pleasure from it. He damn sure showed no remorse over it."

There was a long pause as Beam waited for Daniels to continue.

"Tell me about the Niebel murders," said Beam. "I don't need the details. I already have that. I want to know why you did it."

Daniels' eyes began to wander around the room. Heretofore, he had always boasted and proudly claimed responsibility for the Niebel murders, and, yet, today there was a noticeable reluctance even shame on his part.

"I don't know why," said Daniels.

"Now wait a minute," said Beam. "You clearly admitted killing the Niebels the night of July 21st. You and West had come back to get a guard by the name of Willis Harris who had abused you while you were in prison. You'd been drinking practically all evening. You didn't know where he lived, so you stopped at the Niebel house to get directions. Mr. Niebel told you that Harris lived the next house up the road. You couldn't find any rope to tie them up, so you took them to a cornfield six miles away and shot them in the head. Is that about the way it happened?"

Daniels was wringing his hands, his eyes now staring at the floor. "Yeah, that's about the way it happened."

"Why did you have to shoot them? Couldn't you have simply left them out there in that cornfield? You certainly would have had enough time to have found Harris."

Daniels paused. He stopped fidgeting and turned to Beam. "I don't know."

"So, what you're telling me is that all six murders were justifiable."

"Yeah. I suppose so."

Beam slowly shook his head. His whole body tensed in anger. He leaned forward on his chair until his face was inches from Daniels'. "Mrs. Ambrose is left without a husband and with three kids to raise by herself. Mrs. Smith is still in shock. She is being treated by a doctor who is not sure if she will ever recover from that terrible night. The wife of that truck driver still cries, hysterically, everyday. Since she now has no means of support, she is going to sell her house and move in with her sister. And the Niebels, John, Nolana, and Phyllis all dead, and you sitting here in front of me telling me you don't know why. It's clear to me you have no regard for the sanctity of life, but don't you think you at least owe them that much? I'm most certain that the two surviving members of the family, Russ and Loyal, deserve to know. The city of Mansfield deserves to know. In fact, the whole country deserves to know why you would slaughter three innocent people, and you sit here in front of me and tell me that you don't know."

Beam picked up his notebook and pen and leaned back in his chair. "Mr. Daniels, I will defend you in court with the best of my ability, but I have to tell you that you are the most despicable piece of shit I ever met."

Daniels said nothing.

"By the way, you've smiled haughtily and chewed gum throughout this whole ordeal, and now you stare at the floor and wring your hands. Why the change?"

Daniels looked into Beam's face. From the sound of his voice and the way he emphasized each spoken word, clearly Beam already knew the answer.

"This has all been a part of an act, hasn't it?" asked Beam, his voice now showing anger. "You are trying to convince me that you are now contrite and humbled for what you have done. You want me to feel sorry for you, and maybe, just maybe, I'll try a little harder to defend you. It's no different from the show you put on for the press."

Beam got to his feet and summoned one of the guards to let him out.

"This conversation never happened, Mr. Daniels. We will begin to plan your defense the next time I come back."

Beam waited for the guard to open the cell. He turned to Daniels. The egotistical, smug smile had returned to his face confirming Beam's suspicions.

The guard then opened the door, and Beam marched out of the cell.

***

It was the morning of August 6, 1948. The courtroom was crowded with people standing along the walls and others who had been turned away standing outside. The national exposure had brought hundreds of media people from all around the country to the small town of Mansfield.

It was nearly nine o'clock when a sheriff's car stopped in front of the courthouse. A gathering of hundreds paced restlessly at the front door waiting for Daniel's arrival. Three men dressed in uniforms got out of the car and gathered around the driver's side backdoor. One of the men opened the door, and Daniels got out. They huddled around him to protect him from some would-be assassin and quickly escorted him to the front door.

Once inside, Robert Murl Daniels was led to his seat. He was wearing a brown double-breasted suit with a white shirt and red tie. Acting jittery, he folded and unfolded his manacled hands. Despite his perilous situation, Daniels brandished a haughty, almost unnerving smile that incited anger among many and a strong desire for swift retribution from most everyone who ever met him.

The room was teeming with curiosity seekers and media personnel. There was excitement in the air that was born from a morbid desire for sensationalism. Additionally, there was a sense of accomplishment for the average spectators who had gained admittance to the courtroom despite the overwhelming odds against it.

By nine o'clock, all the seats in the courtroom were filled, and there were other spectators standing against the back walls. The room was filled with a low murmur of talking with an occasional outburst of laughter. Never before had anyone in the area seen such a circus-like atmosphere in that courtroom.

Shortly after nine, Judge G.E. Kalbfleisch entered the room. He took his seat at the bench and called the courtroom to order. Despite the overwhelmingly large crowd, the room fell instantly silent. Kalbfleisch asked for a plea and along with Daniels, his attorney, Lydon H. Beam, stepped before the judge and entered a plea of "not guilty by reason of insanity."

The judge turned to Daniels. "You've heard the statement of your counsel?"

"Yes, sir," said Daniels.

Beam handed the court a paper containing the plea in writing.

After reading the plea aloud, Judge Kalbfleisch asked Daniels, "Is this your wish and desire?"

"Yes, sir," said Daniels.

Judge Kalbfleisch turned to Beam. "You are in effect more accurately saying that you contend he was insane at the time of commission of the crime and that he presently is not insane?"

"Yes, sir, your honor," said Beam.

The judge then asked Beam, "Are you satisfied that this man is of such mental capacity that he fully comprehends the nature of the crime and that he can assist you in every way in preparing his defense?"

"As far as I am able to observe that is a true statement. He has the mental capacity to know the seriousness of the offense."

"Your plea has been entered," said Judge Kalbfleisch. He then banged his gavel. "Next case."

It was nearly a week later that Beam stopped by to see Daniels. There had only been three previous private meetings between the two men. Beam was busy with a full workload, and because of his distaste if not abhorrence for Daniels, he only met with him under extreme necessity.

A guard ushered him through the open door and locked it behind him.

Beam pulled up a chair. "How's it going?"

Daniels smiled. His eyes were slits as if he had been sleeping. "I'm so bored I'm even happy to see you."

Beam smiled. "You should be happy to see me. I'm the only one who stands between you and the electric chair."

"That doesn't sweeten your lousy personality one bit," said Daniels with a smirk.

Beam opened his briefcase and sifted through papers. "Well, now that we have exchanged pleasantries, let's get to work."

"What do you think?" asked Daniels.

"What do I think about what?"

"What do you think of my chances to escape the chair?"

"What makes the difference what I think?"

"It makes all the difference in the world. You just said it. You're the only one who can keep me from going."

"I don't know what your chances are."

"Give me a guess."

"I don't know."

"Give me a guess anyhow."

"One in a million."

Daniels paused then looked away. "I had to ask."

Beam sorted through more papers. "We're going to waive your right to a jury trial."

"What does that mean?"

"Your trial will be heard by three judges instead of a jury."

"Why on earth would I want to do that?"

"You'd be hard pressed to find a soul in this county, state or country for that matter who doesn't hate you and want you to die."

"Don't hold back, Beam ole boy. Tell it like it is."

"There's no possible way you would get a fair trial. Every juror would be biased. The only chance we have is for you to be judged by men who are paid to be impartial, and even then, I have my doubts that they can put aside their feelings."

"So from what you're telling me, I shouldn't figure on too many friends stopping by."

"Mr. Daniels, you're without doubt the most hated man in America," said Beam, with a straight forward almost matter of fact tone of voice. "The last person to attain your infamous stature would have been Adolph Hitler."

Daniels smiled. "I told you this wasn't going to do much for your win-loss record."

Beam closed his briefcase and got to his feet. "See you in court tomorrow."

***

The next day, Beam and Daniels appeared in court at 11:20 in the morning. Beam announced that he wanted to waive trial by jury. He then presented the signed motion, and Kalbfleisch checked it with statutes to see if the form complied with regulations.

The judge turned to Daniels. "Before the court proceeds we wish to ask you if your attorney has discussed this matter with you and want to make sure that you understand your constitutional right to a trial by jury."

Kalbfleisch explained that the constitution provided that only the accused could absolve himself of the right to trial by jury. He added that Daniels could waive today's motion at any time until the trial begins.

"The case will begin and end with three judges, two of whom will be selected by the Chief Justice of the state of Ohio to sit with me," said Kalbfleisch.

The judge then asked Daniels if he had any questions, and he said that he didn't. He then moved the trial back to September 13th to allow time for the appointment of the other two judges.

The next morning began without notice as every morning does in a windowless room. Over the weeks of confinement, Daniels was consumed by the solidarity and eventually lost all sense of time.

Cold metal doors clattered and screeched as they swung on rusted pivots. Daniels looked up from his bed at two figures standing beside him. A guard slammed the door behind them.

"Mr. Daniels, my name is Dr. Bushong, and this is Dr. Bateman."

Daniels sat on the edge of his bed. "Ah, yes. You must be the two doctors who were given the dubious honor of verifying my sanity."

The two men pulled chairs near the bed and sat down.

"Seems a bit strange that you would put it that way," said Bateman. "Why not consider our visit as an attempt to prove your insanity?"

"Come on, gentlemen. We're all adults here. We all know this is just a charade of sorts, a formality to be completed to satisfy all the paperwork and the conscious of those who will send me to my death. After all, you can't fry a crazy man. Crazy people don't know right from wrong. Gotta clear up that matter. We all want to know for sure that the man we are about to kill is sane."

"Interesting observation, Mr. Daniels," said Bushong jotting notes on lined, yellow paper.

Bateman smiled as he listened to Daniels. He immediately recognized that Daniels was more intelligent than he let on. Right now, he was dancing for them, playing mind games that were meant to distract them from the truth. He sensed that Daniels was cunningly leading them down a path that would most certainly suggest that he was at the very least troubled if not insane. He half-heartedly cloaked his true feelings with a pompous and disdainful manner hoping they would conclude that he was purposely hiding a deranged mind. He was obviously of a higher intellect than the average criminal, and which introduced the question of why and how. Why did he do it, and how did his life get this distorted?

"Tell me something, Mr. Daniels," said Bateman.

"Call me Bob, will ya? Nobody has called me that since I was a kid. After all, there's no reason for our being so formal. Wouldn't you say?"

"Okay, Bob. Tell me about your parents."

Daniels smirked. "You're not going for the Oedipus Rex Complex, are you?"

Bateman flashed a quick grin. "I want to know how they get along and generally how they treated you."

Daniels' eyes wandered over the room as he considered the question. "If I had to characterize their relationship, I would have to describe it as one prolonged fight. Can't remember a day when they didn't fight about something. Don't get me wrong. I really do believe they loved one another. In fact, there was no anger during most of the fights."

Daniels jumped. "Oh, my God," he muttered.

Bateman stopped writing in his notebook. "What's wrong, Bob?"

"I used the past tense. I made the reference of when they loved one another. I used the past tense when they are obviously both still alive. I ask both of you gentlemen who are esteemed members of the field of psychology and are trained to interpret such slips of the tongue, what does that mean?"

"What do you think it means?" asked Bateman.

"Good God, I'm just a common, blue-collared laborer. I couldn't possibly be wise and learned enough to explain something as deep and profound as that."

"Come on, Bob," said Bushong. "Take a shot at it. Show us what you're made of."

"Well, let's see," said Daniels grinning and looking away. "I must be thinking in the past tense because, subconsciously, I'm regarding myself as already dead. I'm a walking dead man as they say. My race with mortality is already over in my mind. In other words, it's not my parents living in the past tense, it's me."

There was a pause as the two men scribbled notes.

"How did you do in school, Bob?" asked Bushong.

"Could have done better," blurted Daniels. "I'm a genius, you know or darn near one. Can't remember my I.Q. but it's somewhere high on the scale. Yes, sir, I could have done great if I had just put a little effort in it."

"And why didn't you work at it?" asked Bateman.

"Intelligent people become bored much quicker than average people. School was much too easy for me. I needed something a bit more challenging. Actually, that kind of rhetoric sounds much better than what is more likely the truth, and that is I was just plain lazy. Now, that's a real shame. Here's a guy with an I.Q. off the charts and he's too lazy to use it for good. It doesn't matter how smart you are, you still have to apply yourself. You actually have to get off your lazy ass and do something. When you think about it, it doesn't seem fair. If you're that intelligent, it would seem to me that should be enough. You shouldn't have to work too. Everything should be delivered to you without you ever getting out of bed. If there is a God, why did He create so many lazy people? And why would he invent a smart guy like me with no ambition to use it? You know the common thread of all losers? They're all lazy. Oh, you can be stupid and still succeed. There are a lot of dumb people in high places. What it all comes down to is ambition and drive wins out over intelligence every time."

Daniels stopped and looked at the two doctors. They were busy taking notes.

"I'm just rambling here. Should we head down some other road?" asked Daniels.

Bateman paused and stared at Daniels as if his thoughts would be resurrected by peering into his eyes.

"Let's talk about violence," said Bateman. "You seem to be no stranger to it. How do you feel about violence and have you ever inflicted it upon someone other than the Niebels?"

"Wouldn't you think a man of my I.Q. would rise above such activity? He would have more sense than to take another person's life or hurt someone for that matter. Can't say as I understand it. Maybe if I had taken the time, I wouldn't be in this predicament. Maybe if I hadn't been so lazy, I would have earned my own lunch money for school and wouldn't have had to beat a kid half my age and size nearly to death for a lousy quarter."

Daniels grew increasingly angry. The forever smirk that he wore on his face disappeared.

"Maybe I wouldn't have pummeled his face until it was hamburger. The poor kid was crying when I started hitting him and was silent when I finished. I thought the kid was dead. There was blood all over the place including me. I had to go home and change clothes."

Daniels leaned back. His face was cold. His arrogance had seemingly turned to remorse.

"That was my first time. For some shameful reason I went out of my head. Hell, I felt bad about it later, but I felt nothing while it was happening. How could someone lose their sense of right and wrong and their power of reasoning for a few frightful moments? What I did was disturbing, and, yet, during the blackout that I encountered, I felt nothing.

"That was just the beginning. There were more fights, some for a reason, some for no reason at all. I often wondered why I was like that. Didn't make sense to me. Other guys don't behave like that. They don't need to see someone bleeding to feel better about themselves. And then it hit me. I think it was when I discovered the blackjack. Never before has there been a weapon invented that is quite like the blackjack. It is such a benign, innocuous looking instrument, and, yet, can wield powerful blows to the body that can easily be fatal. The blackjack is simple in design. It is simply a piece of lead wrapped in leather with a handhold fashioned at the other end, and, yet, it will instill fear in just about any man. I fell in love with the blackjack when I realized the power and control I gained by having it. I feared no man, and the best part was no man called me names or pushed me around."

Daniels paused for a moment. "Both of you write this down," said Daniels. "Daniels is guilty of a low self-esteem and compromises by beating people and shooting them thus bolstering his ego. What a sick diagnosis, but I'm sure you'll agree that I'm not far off the mark. In other words, I'm a sick bastard. Please be advised that I say this not to influence your decision as to whether I'm sane or not. In fact, I will make it easy on you and declare that Robert Murl Daniels is quite sane. He just has a few issues regarding his ego. After all, don't we all seek validation of our existence and our equality if not superiority to other humans we encounter? Don't we all need to have our egos stroked to some degree? Doesn't a woman need a man to tell her of her beauty? Doesn't a man need to hear how successful he is to validate his self worth?"

Dr. Bateman held up one hand as if to indicate he wanted to interrupt. "Mr. Daniels, are you attempting to justify to us the crimes you committed?"

"Maybe and maybe not. Maybe my warped criminal brain feels vindicated by such thoughts, or maybe I should be ashamed by comparing my heinous acts of violence with the innocence of the everyday John Doe's problem with his ego."

"Mr. Daniels, or Bob if you prefer, I learned that you're not married and have no steady girl. You are twenty-four years old. Don't you find that a bit unusual?" Bateman asked.

"Does that mean I'm queer?"

"Not necessarily."

"Oh, so what you're saying the possibility exists."

"I didn't say that."

"Well, come right out with it, Mr. Bateman. Do you believe that I am a homosexual?"

"No, I don't."

"You can be truthful with me, Mr. Bateman. As you can see, I am shackled and unable to hurt you."

"Would you hurt me for suggesting that you might be a homosexual if you weren't in manacles?"

"I have beaten men twice my size for suggesting such a thing."

"Why did you beat a man for that?"

"I simply will not allow any man to call me that."

"Why? Is this another one of those ego things?"

Daniels went silent. He smiled in acknowledgement of what was said. "Score one for the doctor," he muttered.

"Back to the issue at hand," said Bateman. "Let's assume that you are not a homosexual. You're a good-looking man, why haven't you had a lasting relationship with a woman?"

"I guess it's because I have such a low opinion of women. I really can't get serious about any of them."

"Why is that?"

"They're so shallow. Their only concern in life is what shade of lipstick they should wear. They are so obsessed with their looks and appearance that they lose track of what's important."

"Well, Bob, surely you understand that looks are important to a woman. It's almost an animalistic gesture to attract a man. It's pretty basic, don't you agree?"

"Actually, Bateman old buddy, you hit the nail right on the head. It's basic stuff. About as basic as you get. I once read there are seven steps or, if you will, layers of attainment, in the life of a human. Basic, primal self-gratification is on the bottom, and as you climb these steps into upper layers, the human involvement and concerns become more sophisticated and more involved with societal issues, and one becomes, more or less, other-oriented. As I remember, the seventh level and last level of concern had to do with mortality and the possibility of an after life. From what I've experienced, women never crawl out of that bottom level. Anything associated with levels two through seven is not worth discussion or consideration. They are forever stuck in that moronic stage of eating, drinking, sleeping, sex and anything else that proves to be self-fulfilling."

"Mr. Daniels, don't you consider that to be a very narrow-minded view of half the population of the earth?"

"Obviously, I shouldn't broad stroke the entire species based on my own personal experiences, so maybe I should correct that by saying every female I have ever known is stuck in level one. It was wrong of me to postulate that all women are the same as what I have encountered."

"Given your opinion of women in general, I'm surprised you don't date women simply to satisfy your basic urges."

"I do, but it seems rather manipulative, don't you agree?"

"How so?"

"Dating a woman just to have sex with her feels like I'm using her for my own personal gain with no regard for her well-being."

"Mr. Daniels, you shot a woman point blank in the head and condemn all others for being socially retarded, yet, you have moral reservations about having sex with them?"

"Seems a bit contradictory, doesn't it?" asked Daniels. "But then again, my whole life has been a series of contradictions, humiliating failures, and unending defeats. I believe if I had had the encouragement of one success or maybe even the encouragement of a parent to try to be successful, I wouldn't be here today."

"Mr. Daniels, do you think you deserve to die for your crimes?" asked Bateman.

Daniels forced a grin. "Yes, and I think the devil has a special place already waiting for me."

There was a long silence as everyone, including Daniels, considered his last statement.

The interview continued for over three hours. With great skill, Daniels tried diligently to deceive the doctors into thinking he was insane or, at least, instill a reasonable doubt. With their testimony and declaration that at the time of the murders he was incapable of determining right from wrong, he would most likely escape his date with the electric chair. He would most likely be transferred to a mental hospital where he would spend time undergoing treatment for mental problems. After a period of time, he could even be released when it was determined that he was no longer a threat to society.

But unfortunately for Robert Murl Daniels, it was not to be. Both doctors positively concluded that he was legally sane, and that they would testify as such. Thankfully, it was an easy conclusion because the public pressure to put Daniels to death was mounting. In light of public sentiment, a decision by Dr. Bateman and Dr. Bushong that would postpone or even stopped Daniels execution would have met with anger and outrage.

Chapter Eighteen

It was September 13, 1948. Fall was only days away, and, yet, the heat of summer was unrelenting. Temperatures soared into the eighties, scorching the hillsides of central Ohio and surrounding areas. With no rain in months, lawns lay dormant with only traces of yellowed and brown grasses. Crops lay in ruin under the late summer sun.

At the edge of the downtown area of Mansfield, a crowd of people stood in front of the Richland County Common Pleas courtroom. It was the first day of the first degree murder trial of Robert Murl Daniels, and the only ones lucky enough to get a seat in the courtroom had formed a line at six o'clock that morning.

The courthouse was built in the late 1800's. It was gothic in its architectural design with great attention to details. In comparison, the courtroom was bland and uninspiring, yet, had ample seating.

The Daniels trial was not the first of a sensational nature conducted in that courtroom. In 1896, and during the same week of the Daniels trial, Celia Rose was tried in that same courtroom for the triple slaying of her mother, father and brother. She was eventually placed in the state hospital in Lima. Then, in 1936, L. H. Beam, the father of Daniels' attorney defended Charles

Wilson in another sensational murder case in the same courtroom. The twenty-two year old Wilson was charged with the murder of his sweetheart, Jean Moorhead, who was by all regards considered to be a prominent citizen of Mansfield.

The crowd, made up almost entirely of women, was orderly that morning, and, yet, there was a pervasive tension that seemed to engulf the room. All the seats were occupied except for a section near the front of the courtroom reserved for special guests and witnesses who were asked to testify. Courtroom etiquette forbade spectators to be standing during a trial, but for this particular event, the restriction was lifted, thus allowing admittance of a few of the town citizenries who were jammed in the hallways and lobby.

Low murmurs and quiet talk filled the room and seemed to add to the growing tension. As special guests and key witnesses entered the courtroom and were seated, the room became silent as everyone tried to identify the players in this high-profile drama and what role they played. Then, as if on cue, the whispering resumed, usually, with more intensity.

It was just about 8:30 when representatives from nine out-of-town newspapers and two press services filed into the courtroom and were seated at a special press table.

Just after they were seated, an uniformed police officer entered the courtroom and took a seat in the reserved section. The spectators soon recognized him as Sargent Lester Conn. He was the Van Wert police officer who was shot by John West when police stopped the pair of killers at a roadblock just outside Van Wert.

At about 8:45, the crowd became quiet. It was an eerie silence, not unlike the silence of a predator stalking its prey. The shackled defendant, Robert Daniels entered the courtroom. Escorted by two armed guards, he was led to his seat at the front of the courtroom. Unaffected by the gravity of the situation and in his usual pompous style, Daniels was chewing gum and smiling at the spectators. Many were shocked at his casual, seemingly, defiant attitude while others were angered and wanted to "slap the grin from his face."

The courtroom was buzzing now. Rumors and stories of all kinds were passed back and forth about the twenty-four year old killer. Very few of the legendary stories were true, most were embellished for the sake of nothing more than sensationalism.

Moments later, a hush fell over the crowd at the unexpected arrival in court of Daniels' father and his sister, Lillian Sims. Cautiously, yet, undaunted, the pair walked down the main aisle to a front row seat near Robert. Daniels turned to his father. He was met with a cold and deliberate stare. No words were said, not even a nod of the head.

Then, as if the American flag was passing, the crowd became completely quiet from one end of the room to the other. Grief-stricken Loyal and Russ Niebel and their wives filed solemnly down to the front row. It was an understatement to say that the whole proceedings had been a trying ordeal for the two young couples. But they remained a courageous calm in the constant presence of the man who had confessed to killing three members of their family.

In an interview, Loyal explained, "We came here to hear the witnesses, particularly the defendant, tell what they knew about the circumstances surrounding the deaths of our family. We have already learned a little more than we knew about the tragedy and hope to have more questions cleared for us by the defendant's testimony."

Then, suddenly, as if on cue, Daniels was led out of the courtroom while photographers were permitted to photograph the pre-trial courtroom. Mr. Daniels and his daughter turned their backs and hid their faces as the photographers snapped picture after picture. When they were finished, Daniels was led back into the room and took a seat next to his lawyer.

It was a few minutes after nine when a door opened at the front of the courtroom, and three men dressed in black robes emerged. They were Judge Pendleton of Findlay, H.E. Culbertson of Ashland, and presiding was Judge G.E. Kalbfleisch of Richland County. They took their places on the bench and called the courtroom to order.

Prosecutor Theodore Lutz, in his opening statement, told the court that "the state will show that the Niebels were killed maliciously, purposely, and with premeditated knowledge."

Lutz was now strutting back-and-forth in front of the panel of judges. His success as a prosecutor was renown with a win loss record that was without equal. With Daniels own confession and the preponderance of evidence mounting against him, Lutz was confident that he would soon have another conviction.

Lutz told the court that Daniels arrived at the Niebel house around one in the morning of July 21st, spent a short time, and then drove the Niebels to the cornfield.

"The evidence will show that after a few minutes, Daniels took a .25 caliber handgun and shot John, Phyllis, and Nolana Niebel, and the evidence will show they died of gunshot wounds."

He then told of their flight to Cleveland. They then fled to Tiffin where they killed Smith and Taylor. He told the court that property belonging to the Niebels was found in the car abandoned by Daniels. Lutz gave a fiery and convincing opening statement that sent waves of head-nodding approvals through the gallery of spectators. He then took his seat, and Beam approached the bench.

In his opening statement, Beam told the court that he would prove that at the time of the crime and immediately before, Daniels was laboring under such an unbalanced mental condition that "He did not understand the nature of his acts, and he did not know right from wrong." Beam said that Daniels' mind was in such a condition that "He was unable to create an act of criminal intent."

Beam said that early in his childhood, Daniels suffered a head and spinal injury and for many months he was unable to move. He said the injury put Daniels in "an unconscious state of mind, and the injury manifested itself later in a lapse of memory."

Beam said Daniels suffered another head injury at the age of thirteen while riding on a bicycle, and was unconscious for several days. "Since the accidents, his acts have to be psychopathic. He has suffered severe headaches, delusions and hallucinations, and lapses of memory."

Beam also told the court that Daniels developed a close relationship with West while they were both in the reformatory. "I expect to show that West was a dominating character and Daniels a willing subject to his influence."

The defense said it would attempt to prove that Daniels was in a demented state at the time of the crime orgy. "This plus the fact that he was out to get Red Harris, a reformatory guard, for alleged rough treatment was responsible for the crime," Beam said.

With a look of confidence and with a voice of assurance, Beam told the court that West started the shooting in the cornfield where the nude bodies of the Niebels were found. "Daniels may have fired shots, but he has no recollection of doing any act towards the Niebels. He was laboring under such a diseased mental condition he didn't know what he was doing. Daniels didn't know right from wrong and did not know the extent of the act he was committing."

Beam finished his statement and returned to his seat. As he walked across the room, the crowd of spectators murmured and stared at him with nearly the same disdain they had for Daniels.

The first witness called to the stand by the prosecutor was Reverend Veler. His testimony was neither dramatic nor sensational in nature. It was merely perfunctory designed to establish that the crime had, indeed, been committed. Veler gave a brief account of finding the bodies and how he called the sheriff from the nearest farmhouse. Beam did not cross-examine the witness, and Veler was dismissed.

At that point, many were shocked as to why Lutz didn't take advantage of the opportunity that Veler presented. Here was an eyewitness to the bloody murder scene. A description of what he saw in that cornfield would have had a great impact and certainly would have been beneficial to the prosecutor by enraging even the stoic, stone-faced judges sitting on the bench.

However, the tactics of the prosecutor became obvious with the announcement of his next witness. He asked that Coroner Lavender come to the stand. It was plain to see that Lutz did not want to dilute the shock value of Lavender's testimony.

The coroner took the oath and sat in the witness chair. Women leaned forward in their seats, and old men cupped their ears to better hear the grizzly details. He began by saying that he arrived at the cornfield shortly after 2:00 in the afternoon of July 21st. He said that he found that Nolana Niebel had been shot in the top of the head and in the abdomen. She also had a bruise on her head made by a blunt instrument. Lavender found that the bullet that killed John Niebel entered the back of the head and emerged at the nostril. He said there was a bruise near the bullet wound.

As Lavender spoke, there were gasps and muttered expletives across the room. Many had heard the grim details of the brutal slayings, but it didn't distract from the shock of hearing the coroner's testimony. The surviving members of the Niebel family were sitting in the front row only a few feet away and listening to the gruesome details. The two women hid their faces as they sobbed while the two men looked on without expressions.

Lavender then testified that the bullet that killed Phyllis Niebel entered her body at the top of her head. Lutz then introduced state's exhibit "B" the bullet taken from the body of Phyllis Niebel. He also introduced as exhibits the separate pictures of the Niebels as they were found in the field.

It was about that time when fifteen-year-old James Edward Mitchell fainted in his seat and fell on the floor. A doctor in attendance rushed to his side to revive him. Later, the boy admitted he had skipped school to attend the trial.

Other witnesses testified for the prosecution that first day. Their testimony had little impact other than establishing the whereabouts of the two killers.

Later in the day, a discussion began that involved the admittance as evidence of a notebook that contained a written confession by Daniels. By the end of the day, a decision had still not been made, so the matter was postponed until day two. Other small matters were addressed, and Judge Kalbfleisch brought the first day of the trial to an end.

The next day, Tuesday, September 14, the crowd outside the courtroom and in the hallways was much smaller, and the mood was much less intense. Many who had failed to get in the courtroom on the first day considered it pointless to try again on the second day.

The trial commenced with the continuation of the debate from the day before. It was important to the prosecutor that the written confession be admitted, otherwise, he would have to rely on circumstantial evidence to get a conviction. It was obvious that the three judges had made their decisions. They impatiently allowed further debate between Lutz and Beam but gave little regard to the arguments presented, and, in fact, soon ended the debate before the participants were finished.

Ultimately, the three judges refused to admit as evidence the notebook containing the hand-written notes of the confession. They did, however, admit three typewritten copies that were signed by Daniels. These were brought into court that day by Merrill A. Mock, staff lieutenant of the state highway patrol, who said he obtained the confession from Daniels shortly after his capture and who would testify against Daniels.

The first witness called to the stand was Everett McSavaney, special investigator for the state bureau of investigation. He said that he heard Daniels tell Mock of how he and West came to Mansfield to get Red Harris because "he gave them a hard way to go." McSavaney went on to say that Daniels said that Niebel was his second choice. The witness quoted Daniels as saying they took the Niebels to a dark road outside Mansfield and told Niebel, "I told you I was coming back to get you."

He said Daniels quoted Niebel as saying, "I've heard that before."

McSavaney related that Daniels said, "Johnnie placed a loaded gun on the kitchen table at the Niebel home, stuck another in his belt and dared Niebel to reach for it."

McSavaney continued addressing the court. "In Celina, Daniels refused to sign a statement because you had enough to electrocute him and that you were trying to make a rat out of him by his taking women out and shooting them."

Attorney Beam asked, "Wasn't this an old-fashioned grilling?"

McSavaney replied, "Oh, no. You are mistaken sir."

Beam asked, "Did you rehearse this before you came to court?"

"I have read over the statements," the witness said.

"Do you recollect Daniels' intent to use a blackjack?" Beam asked.

"He said he changed his mind and decided to kill them," McSavaney said. "Niebel was his second choice."

McSavaney was soon dismissed, and the next witness was called.

Captain Floyd Moon of the state highway patrol was sworn in and sat in the witness chair. He said that Daniels freely talked about the Niebel murders. He quoted Daniels as saying, "I shot Niebel in the head, and he fell face down in the dirt. His daughter said that it wasn't his fault. He only worked for the state. I said I couldn't help it. Niebel was a rotten bastard."

Moon testified that Daniels also admitted to the killing of Mrs. Niebel and her daughter. He had obtained a complete oral confession on a recorder, but it wasn't introduced as evidence.

The next witness called to the stand was Merrill Mock, the staff lieutenant of the state highway patrol. He told the court that Daniels had told him how they had come to Mansfield to get Harris and eventually got Niebel instead.

Lutz asked Mock, "You say Daniels was talkative. Was he jabbering?"

Mock slowly shook his head. "No, I wouldn't say he was jabbering. He seemed to know what he was talking about."

"Didn't you and Daniels have an agreement about deleting something out of the memorandum?" asked Lutz.

"There was nothing to be deleted," said Mock.

"Was there ever any other memorandum?"

"There was a notebook," said Mock. "Daniels had not signed that."

"Did you advise him of his legal rights?" asked Lutz.

"Yes, I did."

"Did you promise he could go ahead and sign it and then delete certain statements?" asked Lutz.

"No, sir. He went ahead and signed it and didn't ask that anything be deleted."

"Would you say he was acting normally and knew what he was doing?"

"Yes, sir," said Mock.

At that point, Judge Kalbfleisch leaned over to Mock. "Did you hear any threats against Daniels intending physical or other harm?"

"No, sir," said Mock, and he was then dismissed.

Another witness called was Sheriff Roy Shaffer of Van Wert County. He testified that he climbed to the top tier of the auto transport truck where he found Daniels in the front seat of the first car holding a pistol in each hand and a rifle in his lap. Shaffer said he ordered Daniels to drop his guns, and Daniels complied. He quoted Daniels as saying, "You got me. Don't kill me. I'll do anything you say." Shaffer also said that he found a .25-caliber automatic in Daniels' hip pocket."

Shaffer was dismissed and day two of the trial came to an end.

***

The next morning, Daniels was driven to the courthouse. Manacled to a deputy sheriff, he was escorted inside. Two teenage girls had managed to slip through the crowds to get a glimpse of Daniels. As he walked by them, he turned and smiled. One girl nudged the other ecstatic at the recognition from the young man accused of murder.

The trial began with defense attorney Theodore Beam calling family members of Daniels to the stand. His mother and father testified as well as his sister. His brother Clarence said he took Daniels to the hospital when he was injured at the age of six. He said after the accident, his brother "didn't have any pep. He just sat around."

Beam asked him if he saw his brother after he was released from the reformatory, and he said he did.

"Did he show any unusual conduct?" asked Beam.

"In talking and acting, I thought he was going crazy," said Clarence.

One of the most significant testimonies during the third day of the trial was when Dr. Bateman and later when Dr. Bushong testified.

"Do you think he knew right from wrong?" asked the prosecutor.

"I think he was able to," said Bateman.

"Do you think he knew the nature of the crime he was committing?"

"Yes, I think he knew."

Then the doctor added, "The statement he made to me showed remorse." He opened his notes and quoted from Daniels. "I regretted it awful after it was over. I said to Johnnie, 'I shouldn't have killed the girl. Why the girl? She was too young, and the mother too."

"Did he express remorse over killing Mr. Niebel?"

"Not at all," said the doctor.

Then it was Beam's turn to question the doctors. He asked if three and one-half hours was long enough for a psychiatric examination.

"Yes, I think so," said Bateman. "Mental examinations in probate court require three to seven minutes and rarely over fifteen minutes."

Beam then recalled some of Daniels' actions and asked if they were hallucinations.

Dr. Bateman said, "What you have related is a delusory imagination, the result of a guilty complex, a very common thing."

"Did you see any tendency to psychosis?"

"None, whatsoever."

"Did you find any evidence or anything that would indicate a mental disorder?"

"No, sir. I did not," was the doctor's reply.

"Thank you, Dr. Bateman," said Beam. "You are dismissed."

To the surprise of many, Robert Daniels took the stand and without hesitation and with a touch of pride, he announced to the court at 11:45, "I believe I killed the Niebels to a certain extent, but as far as certain knowledge I can't say I did. Well...I don't know. I can't remember. I can't say. I can't remember seeing the Niebels fall."

After making that statement, Daniels even identified the .25-caliber pistol that killed Phyllis Niebel as the gun he held on the Niebels while they drove them to the cornfield.

Earlier in his testimony, Beam asked him about his early injuries and school days. His answers were somewhat vague and illusive. Daniels seemed to show interest when Beam began to ask him about his crime career.

"Do you remember being in Lancaster?"

"Yes."

"When you left Lancaster, where did you go?"

"Home."

"Did you get into any trouble after that?"

"I was involved in a robbery with some friends. I was about 19 or 20 at the time."

"What happened after the armed robbery after you were apprehended?"

"I went to the Mansfield Reformatory for about three or four years."

"What did they have you doing?"

"I worked in the shoe shop and then in the furniture shop. Later I worked two different times on the farm. I then worked in the horse barn. I drove a team of horses and my duties were to curry and brush the horses. Everyday, Harris would show up at the barn and give me orders for the day."

"You worked for Red Harris?"

"Yes."

"Red Harris gave you orders for the day?"

"Yes."

"Did you know John Niebel?"

"I saw him out there. He was superintendent of the farm. I didn't know him very well."

"Can you remember an occasion when you tried to harness the team and found that articles were missing?"

"One morning, I couldn't find the harness and bridle. I looked everywhere for them but couldn't find them, so I told Harris."

"What did he do?"

"Harris always hollered at me and called me every name in the book. That morning, he found the bridle and hit me with it about three or four times. He hit me so hard, I got a knot on my head and had to go to the hospital."

"Did you have any more trouble with Harris?"

"I once told Harris that a wagon was broken and couldn't be used. He threw a club at me."

Daniels went on to tell the court about his crime spree that began with the murder of the bar owner, Earl Ambrose. It was only a few days later that they made the trip to Mansfield to get even with Red Harris.

"I was going to get Red Harris, and Johnnie wanted to get some other guard out there. I don't remember his name. This guard busted Johnnie's head with a club."

"When did you arrive in Mansfield?"

"I don't remember times and dates. Of course, I was drinking some."

"What happened then?"

"We went to the Ringside Night Club because we knew that Harris hung out there."

"Did you try to find Harris?"

"Neither one of us knew where he lived so Johnnie got a bunch of nickels and started calling all of the Harrises in Mansfield."

"When did you go out to the Niebel house?"

"That night, I guess."

"Remember going out there?"

"Yes, I remember."

"How did you happen to go to the Niebels?"

"We wanted to find out about Harris and about this other guard. We went out there to find out where these two guards lived."

"How did you decide to go there?"

"We knew him being the superintendent of the farm he would know where these guards lived. He told us."

"Did he tell you where Harris lived?"

"He told us where Harris lived. He lived the next house up. I remember that."

"Did you discover other members of the Niebel family?"

"Yes, there were three of them altogether."

"What happened then?"

"We wanted to tie them up, but we didn't have any rope, so we took them down in the basement."

"Remember what you did in the basement?"

"We were going to tie them up in the basement. We were looking for rope. Anyhow, we couldn't tie them up."

"Did you take them out of the basement?"

"I held a gun on them, Johnnie's rod."

"Where did you go?"

"We went out to a cornfield."

"Can you locate that now?"

"If you put me on a road that leads to Cleveland, I think I can. If I was on it, I think I can take you out there."

"What happened at the cornfield?"

"We led them out into the cornfield and made them take off their clothes."

"Why did you make them take off their clothes?"

"So that we would have time to go back and get Harris."

"What happened then?"

"We didn't have any rope. Johnnie wanted to shoot them. I told him no, take them out and tie them up. There wasn't any rope, and I was standing in front of Mr. Niebel. I remember Johnnie pulling a trigger on a gun. It all got kind of crazy, but I do remember the Niebels being lined up and the next day I was some place with Johnnie...Cleveland."

"What happened after that?"

"And Johnnie said you got more than I have. He told me I had killed all three of the Niebels starting with Mr. Niebel first. I told Johnnie I could remember that I was there, and, by the way, several times I have awakened and found myself some place, and I don't know how I got there. That's happened to me several times."

"You have no recollection of firing the shots?"

"I can't truthfully say I fired the shots. I had a faint recollection of firing a shot. There is a possibility."

"Do you remember how you got out of the cornfield?"

"I was driving. I remember coming to the end of the road. I turned to the right and I drove and that's when I realized I was driving. I knew the directions to Cleveland."

"Did you have any conversation with Phyllis in the cornfield?"

"She didn't say anything in the cornfield, but at the house, she said that her dad can't help it if he works for the state."

"Do you remember any conversation with Mr. Niebel?"

"Just when I told him that he had three minutes to get right with the Lord."

Daniels was on the stand for over three hours. Most everyone in the courtroom found him to be illusive, a purveyor of double talk and lies, and disrespectful, if for no other reason than his insistence on chewing gum in a court of law. Despite all that, he did admit guilt to the crimes. If there was any doubt in the mind of anybody who was present in that courtroom as to the outcome of that trial, it was soon cleared up after Daniels freely admitted to virtually every accusation.

The next day was Thursday the 16th. It was the fourth day of the trial, and both the prosecution and defense had presented evidence and witnesses, and it was time for closing statements. There was a tension in the air that seemed to feed the drama that had unfolded and was now coming to fruition. Both Lutz and Beam nervously awaited their last chance to make pleas to the three judges, while Daniels sat calmly chewing his gum.

As prosecutor, Theodore Lutz was first to approach the bench and summarize the state's charges against the defendant. He walked slowly across the room and stopped in front of the bench.

"It is hardly necessary to repeat those things that have been said by the defense. The testimony has been hot and cold and included denials and affirmations that are to be expected in any trial. The defense, however, has said they find no quarrel with the state's case not even in the matter of proving the firearm, the .25-caliber gun, which was state's exhibit "P" and the six empty shell cases. The fact that these people were living was proven by the testimony of Loyal Niebel. We proved that their deaths resulted from bullets fired from state's exhibit "P". The state has proven its case by the exhibits alone and there has been no attempt to contradict this evidence. The defendant himself said, 'I believe I shot them' and with state's exhibit "P".

Lutz said the only accolade in the trial went to Richland County Sheriff Frank Robinson who "deserved the praise he got." Lutz also complimented Defense Counsel Lydon Beam who "did what he could with nothing to work on." Lutz lauded the officers for apprehending what somebody has called, 'mad dog killers'."

The prosecutor characterized the defendant as a spoiled brat on several occasions.

"The court will remember that on four or five occasions on the stand that the answers of the state's questions were barely touched in cross-examination. The defense had the right to refute this testimony but they relied on the defendant to come to the stand to refute one or two minute details."

Lutz described both Dr. Bateman and Dr. Bushong as "both eminent in their field" and thanked them for establishing the sanity of the defendant.

"And I would like to remind the court that no witness at any time testified that the defendant did not know right from wrong or know the consequences of his act."

Lutz paused and then continued, "The defense did not ask for mercy or make any plea on behalf of the family or the 'boy' as they called him. He is 24 years old and has enjoyed all the privileges of manhood a long time. Phyllis was only 21. She had the right to live, to marry and have children."

The six members of the Niebel family, two sons, their wives and two aunts, sat with bowed heads during this part of Lutz's presentation.

Lutz said, "Phyllis' final plea for her father fell on insensitive ears as she lay in the nakedness of maidenhood. She was regarded with nothing but cruel eyes."

Lutz turned to the three-judge panel. "I think the state has proven without any doubt that Robert Murl Daniels is guilty and should be put to death."

There was stillness in the courtroom as many thought about what was said and others regained their composure. In its entirety, it was a very stirring and heart-wrenching speech. Lutz said what many wanted to, but couldn't. They had neither the platform from which to speak as he did nor the narrative skills.

Lutz finished his closing statement and took a seat. It was now time to hear the defense attorney's closing statement. Beam walked across the floor and stood in front of the three judges.

"You've heard Mr. Daniels testify of conditions that exist at the reformatory and about a guard named Harris, a guard who was recently released from the Ohio Sate Penitentiary. He was put in charge of boys too young to be in the penitentiary. You heard Daniels tell of the mental and physical abuse. There is no human being who can take abuse and doesn't want to fight back. It caused a fixation in his mind. Daniels wanted to get even, but he didn't intend to kill Harris.

He said that when they visited the Niebel house and found out he had a family, they took them out to the cornfield to tie them up. It was then that West said, "Let's shoot them."

Beam told the court that Daniels said, "We don't need to do that. We can put them out with a blackjack. That's why we told them to bow their heads, but West started to shoot. The next thing I knew we were on our way to Cleveland."

Beam paused, and then said, "I think you'll find that he's not a mad dog killer as he has been called. I took over the case with considerable misgiving. I have had to be sincere as I proceeded with this case. I have become convinced the defendant is not normal. He is not a killer. He is a poor befuddled-minded boy. Some of the testimony given by the parents and relatives of the accused youth were sincere statements which lead us to believe that this boy was incapable of judging right from wrong and the probability that his mental condition at the time of the crime was one of insanity."

Beam also attacked the testimony of the two court-appointed psychiatrists. "They did not take enough time to examine the youth. You can't cover a man's life in five hours. They're state employees. They are a part of the great scheme of law enforcement. The family had no money or means to employ their own psychiatrist. There is a possibility that their conclusions were not correct. Statements of the family proved that the boy was of unsound mind, and because of his diseased mind, I don't believe he knew right from wrong."

Beam turned to the crowd and singled out four individuals. He said that when Shaffer captured Daniels, he moved in as "the master of ceremonies." He said Shaffer told a story of capturing "this big bad man," but that Daniels meekly surrendered.

"It was certainly a Roman holiday for the police. They were not there in ones, twos or threes to question him. They were there in dozens."

Beam declared that McSavaney was a "smart aleck," that Mock deliberately withheld information, and that Moon used an old police trick of waking up Daniels in the middle of the night when his mind was dead and hammering questions at him.

Beam said the only sincere and honest testimony given by any law enforcement officer was that of by Frank Robinson.

"His was honestly and sincerely given," Beam said.

He added that Robinson admitted they had problems determining by which street they reached the road to Cleveland during the reenactment, so he put him on the road to Cleveland to get to the cornfield.

Beam chastised a few others then closed his statement.

Judge Kalbfleisch adjourned the trial for the day.

Later that evening, A reporter and a photographer were allowed to interview Daniels. As they started up the stairway, an older woman and a young woman met them as they were coming down the stairs. It was Daniels mother and sister. Mrs. Daniels struck the photographer in the back with her purse. "I'll teach you to take pictures of me," she said. Daniels' sister screamed obscenities at him for trying to get pictures of the family since the trial opened.

Daniels was eating a Limburger cheese sandwich that his mother had brought him, when the two men entered the room.

"I'm sure I'll burn," said Daniels. "Those judges will probably give it to me, but I don't think I deserve it. I don't even deserve life in the pen. All the points have not been brought out about my mental condition. Most of my testimony on the stand is damn near a blank to me. I can only remember answering three or four questions and they tell me I was testifying for over two hours."

Daniels' stare drifted to the floor. He slowly shook his head. "I was pretty sure right along that I would burn, and now I'm certain of it."

Daniels was silent after that. The two men tried desperately for another hour to get him to talk but to no avail. The smug, defiant look was gone from his face, replaced by a distinct look of fear.

It was Friday, September 17, 1948. The stage was set for a drama the likes of which Mansfield or the state of Ohio for that matter had never known. Anybody who had followed the trial was convinced of the outcome and were anxious to have it confirmed. Not only was it a Mansfield drama, it was the center of attention in newspapers across the country.

It was about 1:30 in the afternoon when Judge Kalbfleisch, Judge Culbertson and Judge Pendleton filed into the courtroom and took their seats. There was a quiet tension in the air. Both the prosecution and the defense had presented their cases, and now the fate of Robert Daniels was in the hands of the panel of judges.

As it had been the case all week long, the surviving members of the Niebel family were sitting in the front row. Daniels' parents, sisters and brother had all returned to Columbus the night before at Daniel's request, leaving only an uncle, Joseph Daniels of Columbus to hear the verdict.

Before officially opening the session, Kalbfleisch thanked the crowd for "the preservation of order" throughout the trial, adding that he didn't "want any demonstration" when sentence was pronounced.

The judge shuffled some papers and called the court to order. He paused and turned a cold stare at Daniels. "Will the defendant please rise?"

Daniels got to his feet. For the first time all week, he was not wearing a suit and tie and was not chewing gum. His hands trembled and his legs shook.

It was 1:38, when Judge Kalbfleisch read from a small piece of paper. "Robert Daniels, the state of Ohio finds you guilty of first degree murder for the deaths of John Niebel, Nolana Niebel and Phyllis Niebel. A wave of mumbling and murmuring spread across the room. "Do you have anything to say before sentence is passed?"

"I've got a lot to say," said Daniels. "I would like to have my handcuffs removed when I make my statement."

The judge nodded at the deputy who removed his shackles.

"I doubt in my own mind that I committed first degree murder," said Daniels. "The psychiatrists don't know if I was under mental strain. They don't know about me. I don't know myself. I only know what Johnny told me afterwards.

"If I was sure I shot them and saw them fall, I believe I deserve the electric chair. I never killed anything. Until I'm convinced in my own mind, I'll feel that I didn't deserve the chair. I know how I'd feel if my mother, father and sister were killed at one time. That's awful!"

The judge patiently waited until Daniels was finished, then said, "Robert Daniels, you have been found guilty of first degree murder. I sentence you to death in the electric chair at the Ohio Penitentiary on January 3, 1949." He paused. "I will ask Sheriff

Frank Robinson to turn the prisoner over to the penitentiary within thirty days."

The manacles were reattached to his wrists, and he was led out of the courtroom.

That night Robert Daniels sat in his cell staring at the cold concrete and the hardened steel bars. He had finally come to realize that this was a portent of things to come. It was bad enough knowing he had only weeks to live, but to spend his last days in isolation and in such a dreadful environment seemed to be more than ample punishment. For the first time in his life, Daniels sobbed, uncontrollably, all night long. The fright of what lay ahead was now an overwhelming reality. Without realizing it, at one point during the night, he urinated in his pants and lost control of his bowels.

For the city of Mansfield and surrounding communities, life returned to normal after the weeklong trial. Children played outside again even after dark. Houses were left unlocked, and keys left in cars. It had been a harrowing summer, one that nobody would ever forget. It left scars that would last well into the next century.

For everyone else in the world, each day began and ended as a natural way of things. The sun would rise in a spectacular array of colors and set in the west in a similar manner. For Robert Daniels, each day brought him that much closer to his destiny. Days began to blur into one long day without a beginning and without an end. Nothing changed for him. He sat on the edge of his bed staring at the concrete and steel day after day until the concept of a day had no meaning to him. There were no windows in his small world to mark the passing of another day, not even a calendar to track his remaining time on earth.

For many, isolation from the world and human contact can be a torturous experience, and Robert Daniels was no exception. Bill Bailey, the guard assigned to bring Daniels his meals, not only knew John Niebel and his family but considered him a friend as well. He was a veteran with many years of experience and was well aware of the mind-altering agony of isolation. He knew from experience that Daniels would soon be crying out for human contact, a conversation, or a discussion. He would even settle for a friendly smile.

To further along Daniels' descent into hell, Bill Bailey, purposely, delivered the meals while Daniels was asleep. Daniels soon realized what Bailey was doing. He wasn't sure of his motive, but he was aware that this guard was deliberately avoiding him.

As the days passed, Daniels became starved for human contact. He decided to fake sleep to catch Bailey as he sneaked in his meal. Unfortunately for Daniels, Bailey would open the door, slide the tray of food through an opening near the floor and leave the room without verbal exchange or even eye contact with the prisoner.

Soon, Daniels became enraged at these behavioral tactics and would try his best to goad Bailey into saying something. There were three meals delivered by a human being with only seconds involved. At first, Daniels tried a friendly approach with no results. He would offer a greeting only to see the retreating backside of his visitor. Then, as Daniels became angry at this obviously rude tactic, he taunted Bailey with profanity and references to his mother's moral character. Bailey remained unaffected, and, in fact, moved at an even faster pace.

In spite of his intentions, Bailey, most likely, rendered a kindness to Daniels. Instead of the long endless days of staring at the walls, Daniels was now entertained with a diversion, an infuriating diversion, but a diversion none the less.

Chapter Nineteen

Robert Daniels was allowed to see the light of day one more time in his life. On October 10th, he was transferred to the Ohio State Penitentiary in Columbus. For 55 minutes, he could watch the world go by as he stared out the window of the speeding car. Dark gray clouds rolled ominously across the sky warning of things to come. He saw children bundled in warm jackets as they made their way to school. An old man raked leaves in his front yard, and a tractor lumbered down a country road. The last thing he saw as he entered the penitentiary was a pair of doves sitting on the branch of an oak tree.

The Ohio Penitentiary was built in 1834. In 1885, the penitentiary became the site for executions, which had been carried out by local law enforcement officials up to that time. At first, prisoners condemned to death were executed by hanging, but in 1897 the electric chair replaced the prison's gallows.

In the early twentieth century, the Ohio Penitentiary and other prisons in Ohio began to come under attack. Conditions within the facility were not good, and the public view of prisons was beginning to change. In addition, there were problems with bribery, and prisoners with connections received better treatment than the rest. After the fire in 1930, which killed over three hundred inmates, there were even more demands for prison reform. Most of the changes took place after World War II, although reforms did not come quickly enough to keep three prison riots from occurring. Attention was paid to conditions of overcrowding in the post-war years, but prison morale was also a very serious issue.

On the east wing was a small, dedicated area called death row. It housed the few men who were not only waiting to be executed, but whose time was near.

Two guards led Daniels up a flight of stairs and opened a door. There was a long walkway with cells on both sides. Each cell was made of cold-steel bars and only housed one man. They walked him down the corridor to the last cell on the left where they removed his shackles and locked him in his own cell. Once again, he was confined where there were no windows, however, at least this time he wasn't alone. In the cell directly across from his was a man near forty years of age. He was bent over a small desk writing in a spiral ring notebook.

"What's your name?" asked Daniels.

The man didn't speak. He didn't even look up from his work.

"I said what's your name?" said Daniels with a loud voice.

With a look of exasperation, the man removed his glasses and turned his chair to face Daniels. "Is it important?"

Daniels smiled sheepishly. "Well, I guess not, but seeing as how you're going to be the last person I'll ever meet, it might be nice to know your name."

"Chad."

"Chad what?"

"Chad Smith."

"My name is Robert Daniels."

"Didn't ask."

"What did you say?"

"I said I didn't ask your name because I don't care."

The smile on Daniels' face disappeared. "You're in a pissy mood."

"What did you expect?"

"Well, we're both in the same boat, you know. We're both going to die real soon."

"That doesn't mean I have to like you."

Daniels sat on the edge of his cot and slowly shook his head. "Just my luck. I get to spend the last days of my life with a shithead."

"What did you call me?"

"A shithead."

"I guess I deserved that."

"Why do you have to be like that?"

"This ain't the Hilton, buddy."

Daniels paused. "What are you in here for?"

"What does it matter?"

"I guess it doesn't matter at all. I just wanted to talk to someone. I've been in isolation for what seems to be years."

Smith smiled and pointed at Daniels. "I know who you are. You're the guy, who killed that family in Mansfield, aren't you?"

"That's me," said Daniels with his head held high.

"Jesus, you act like you're proud of it."

"Yeah, I suppose I am. Why?"

"You killed two women, didn't you?"

"Yeah."

"What did they do to you to deserve that?"

"Nothing."

"Be glad that you didn't go to prison."

"Why is that?"

"Whether you know it or not, prisoners have certain codes and standards. Killing women violates one of those standards."

"So, what does that mean?"

"You can't guess?"

"I suppose that means I would get a good spanking."

"Oh, you'd get a good one alright."

"Sorry, but I'm not impressed."

"Did you really shoot those three point blank in the head?"

"Yeah. Why?"

Smith slowly shook his head. "I just can't believe anybody would do such a thing. Think about it. How could you pull the trigger on innocent women? You're disgusting. You must have been born from the bowels of the earth."

Daniels gritted his teeth. "So, you're pretty much holier than I am. What, may I ask, are you in here for? Who did you murder?"

"I didn't murder anybody."

"Then, what the hell are you in here for?"

"Rape."

"Rape?" asked Daniels with a surprised look. "They fry you for rape?"

"They're frying me for it."

"Did you do it?"

"What makes the difference? The court thinks I did."

"I don't care what the court thinks. I want to hear your side of it. Did you do it?"

"If the truth be known, no, I didn't rape her."

"Well, then, tell me what happened."

Smith paused. "I'm not so sure I want to talk about it."

"Hey, it's not like we got that much going on right now."

"Good point. Her name was Martha. Damn, she was cute little thing. Couldn't have weighed a hundred pounds and as pretty as a picture. We'd been dating kinda on a regular basis. You know, getting to know one another. After a few months, I was picking up signals that she wanted to get married. Unfortunately, the more I got to know her, the more I knew that she wasn't right for me. Like I said, she was a cute thing, but, my God, she wanted to control everything I did or said."

"Let me guess," said Daniels with a smile. "You dumped her, and she got back at you by yelling rape."

"That's about the size of it."

"I don't believe it. You're about to be strapped into the electric chair because some young girl didn't get her way."

"I guess it's true what they say," said Smith.

"What's that?"

"Hell hath no fury like the wrath of a woman."

"Did you ever have sex with her?"

"No."

"You're going to die for rape, and you didn't even get laid?"

"Now, do you see why I'm a bit touchy?"

"Do you think she'll come to her senses and come forward with the truth?"

"I'm hoping."

"When is your date with the chair?"

"Day after tomorrow."

"Oh, my God. You're down to your last two days, and your only hope is that she will tell the truth! I hate to say it, my friend, but you're screwed."

Smith said nothing.

"I can't believe you're so calm about it. If that had been me, I'd be crazy with anger."

"What infuriates me is that we have a law whereby a man can be put to death for rape. Granted, that's a horrible crime, but is it any worse than shooting a man? My God, you can send a piece of lead tearing through a body destroying organs and possibly making him an invalid, but as long as he lives, they won't put you to death. I hear that there is a state that has a law on the books that if you desecrate a grave it is a capital crime. Imagine that. Go to the electric chair for pushing over a few tombstones."

"Did this girl have any evidence against you?"

"Not a bit. In fact, she waited three days before turning me in."

"Damn, you must have had one bad lawyer," said Daniels.

"Court-appointed and fresh out of law school."

"What are you going to put on your tombstone?"

"What?"

"Your tombstone should have something catchy on it."

"Like what?"

"I don't know. Something like, I got screwed, and she didn't."

Smith smiled, then laughed out loud. Soon he was laughing hysterically wiping tears from his eyes. "Oh, my God, that's funny. That's the first time I've laughed at anything in months. Thanks, Daniels."

"Don't mention it."

Smith turned and stretched out on his bed. "It's time to get some sleep."

"Good God, man. It's about noon."

"Doesn't matter," said Smith. "Not in here, anyhow."

Over the next two days, Smith and Daniels became good friends. Their common bond was their shared destiny, and Smith's destiny was only an hour away. It was 7:00 on October 12th. Smith was scheduled to die at eight.

"Are you okay?" asked Daniels.

Smith had his head in his hands staring at the floor. He said nothing.

"Smith, are you alright?"

"Leave me alone," muttered Smith.

"You haven't said anything for an hour."

Smith retched violently onto the floor.

Daniels smiled. "There goes your last meal. Does that mean you get another one?"

Smith wiped his mouth with his shirtsleeve. "I'm scared, man, scared shitless."

The smile on Daniels' face disappeared as he thought about his own destiny and how he will feel when it's his time. Any chance for a pardon from the governor?"

"Are you kidding me?"

"How 'bout what's-her-name? She can't just sit back and let you go to the chair."

Smith vomited again. He cleaned his mouth with a sock that was lying on the floor. "Dear God, I don't want to die," he said, his voice crackling.

Daniels said nothing.

Smith wiped tears from his eyes. "Any man who tells you he ain't scared to die is a fool. Smith began to sob openly. "I just know that when that door opens, I'm going to shit myself. I just know it. How humiliating. I have to go to my death sitting in my own shit."

Daniels was dazed, struck with fears of his own. He slumped on the edge of the bed staring at the doomed man across the aisle.

"Oh, Christ," said Smith. "I just pissed my pants. God, I'm scared. I wish it didn't have to be this way. I've always been scared of electricity. I remember when I was a little kid I got a shock. You don't soon forget an experience like that. Swore I'd never let that happen again."

Daniels glanced at his hands. They were trembling. His legs were shaking.

"Sorry," said Smith. "I just can't seem to get control of myself. You know, they shave your head before they do it. Shave a part of your leg too. It has something to do with getting a better connection between the metal shackles and your skin. It can be damn ugly if that 2,000 volts doesn't flow properly. Damn ugly.

"One of the guards asked me the other day if I believed in God. I couldn't believe it. Do you really think God would let this happen? I guess I should ask for forgiveness for my sins. Shouldn't take any chances. What do you think? Should I ask Him to forgive me?"

Daniels said nothing.

"Daniels, talk to me."

"I don't know, man. I don't know," Daniels muttered.

The room went quiet. There was just the soft sobbing of Smith as he held his head with his hands.

Suddenly, there was the cold sound of a large metal key clattering inside a steel door. Four men dressed in guard uniforms and a priest entered the room. In unison, they walked over to Smith's cell and opened it.

One of the guards gently laid a hand on Smith's shoulder. "It's time," he said.

Smith wiped his face with the back of his hand and struggled as he got to his feet. He threw his head back and stood straight. A guard took him by the arm, and they all started across the room. The priest muttered softly as he read from the Bible.

"Bye," muttered Daniels to no one in particular.

As they disappeared out the door, Daniels turned to the clock on the wall. It was 7:41. The man had 19 minutes to live. There was still time. Maybe the governor will call at the last minute. It happens in the movies all the time. Maybe that girl will finally do the right thing. Nobody could stand by while a man is executed when you have the power to stop it. She must have a conscious. She must care.

"Oh, my God," said Daniels out loud. He gave a quick glance around the room. "That means that when they come for me, I'll only have 19 minutes to live. Oh, dear God. Of course, that's only if they fry Smith at 8:00. They might be a little late. Maybe a few problems strapping him in or something. It might be 8:05. I gotta check the clock when it happens. I've heard the lights dim. Hope that's true, so I know when it happens. I have to know. Oh God, I wish I had it all to do over. How could I have done such an evil thing as that? What in the world was I thinking? I should have blackjacked them like I planned. There was need to shoot them like that. It was Johnnie's fault. If he hadn't been there, I never would have done it. I was showing off. That's what I was doing. Why else would I do something like that?"

Daniels turned to the clock. It was a minute past eight.

"I knew it," he said with a loud voice. "I knew it would be some time after eight. Nobody ever does anything on time, especially the government."

He turned to the clock. It was now three minutes after eight.

Daniels began to laugh hysterically. "Oh, my God. She must have come to her senses. Old Smith ain't gonna fry after all. There is justice in the world. They'll be bringing him back here to his cell any time now. I'll bet we'll have a good time over this one. Yes, sir, there is justice in the world after all."

It was about that time that the lights dimmed for three seconds. They came back on for another two seconds and then dimmed again for another three seconds. Daniels slowly turned to the clock. It was 8:06.

Ten minutes later, two guards came into Smith's vacant cell. Without respect or regard for a man who had lived a rich full life and had been unmercifully executed by the State of Ohio, they went about their callous duty of cleaning the room. They rolled up the bedding on his cot, ripped down the clippings and photos taped on the walls and finally removed the last remnants of Mr. Smith's life.

Chapter Twenty

The month of October spilled into November and November became December. Daniels watched the days go by with little or no concern. It was if he had taken up residence in his cell and had totally dismissed his impending doom. There was nothing for him to do, and the isolation was beginning to affect his mind. A guard was kind enough to bring him day-old newspapers for his amusement. Not only could he keep up with world events, he could enjoy the approaching Christmas season through the advertisements.

The guard's name was John Miller. He was an older man with only months until retirement. For forty-one years, he had worked for the reformatory in one capacity or another going from one job to another. Mr. Miller did accept one promotion, but all of the other moves were lateral ones. Often he would say, "I need to be here around these fellers. There just might be something I can do for one of them." He didn't actually approve of Daniels or what he had done, but he did feel pity for the young man. A young man who was capable of committing such an atrocity had to have, at the very least, been misled as a child, and, in all likelihood, the boy was exposed to less than ideal role models.

It was Christmas Eve. The end was fast approaching for Daniels, and every day that passed made him more aware of his destiny. It was nearly six o'clock, when Miller brought him his dinner. He slid the tray of food through an opening under the bars and stood straight.

"Merry Christmas," Miller said handing a small present to Daniels.

He took the gift and for several moments stared at it in awe. "I don't believe it," he muttered.

Miller was beaming. "Well, open it."

Daniels tore off the red and green paper and opened the box. Inside was a small glass dome about the size of a man's hand. Daniels shook it, and snowflakes swirled inside and slowly almost hypnotically settled on top of a snowman. He shook it again and watched as a violent snowstorm quickly dissipated and came to rest only to be revived to suffer the same fate.

"That was very kind of you, John," said Daniels, with a broad smile. "I really appreciate it."

Miller blushed. "Everyone should get a little something for Christmas, don't you think?"

Daniels studied the small toy turning in all directions. "I haven't had a toy for Christmas since I can remember. Seems like all I ever got was underwear and socks."

"Everyone should get a toy for Christmas; at least, that's what I always thought."

"Wish you had been my dad."

"Well, like the missus said, even a godless man like you should share in Christ's birthday."

As soon as he had spoken the words, Miller realized he had said something that was somewhat offensive. There was an uncomfortable pause, then Miller said, "Sorry."

"That's okay," said Daniels with a smile. "Thank the missus for me and tell her that she's absolutely right."

"Well, guess I'd better be going," said Miller. "Got some last minute shopping to do for the missus? Don't know why I always wait until the last minute. Every year I swear I won't wait this long, but here I go again just like clockwork."

Miller smiled and thrust his hand through the bars. "Merry Christmas, Mr. Daniels," he said.

Daniels took his hand and slowly shook it. "Merry Christmas to you, Mr. Miller."

Daniels picked the tray of food off the floor, while the old man ambled out the door.

It was just after midnight, officially Christmas Day, when Daniels picked up his present. He shook the toy and watched as the snow settled onto the smiling snowman. A tear streaked down his cheek as he remembered a Christmas long ago. His dad actually borrowed money to buy presents, and for the first time in his life, Daniels opened presents that were not clothes. Later, the entire Daniels family would meet at Grandma's for dinner and family conversation. It was a sweeter time, all those years ago. It was a time of snowball fights, sleds careening downhill, and sleigh rides. In the summer, there were the night sounds of crickets and far-away croaking frogs, of blue skies with fluffy white clouds. He remembered fishing off the banks of a muddy river, protected by an elm tree from the hot morning sun.

It was a wondrous time, a time of innocence and fun. Those days vanished though, lost into the ages, moments captured on a faded, dog-eared photograph and locked forever in a memory.

Daniels carefully placed the toy on a table by his bed, bowed his head and cried.

New Years came and went with no fanfare and even less interest for Daniels. Tension and stress mounted every hour as he waited for January 3rd. He paced his cell wringing his hands and stopping every so often to retch onto the floor. The passage of time had always meant so little for a young man in his twenties. Now, the second hand on the clock was the enemy, relentlessly, racing in its never-ending circular path. He wanted to stop it. Make it quit. Stop time even if it meant a lifetime in this small cubicle.

It was early evening just after 7:00. The prison priest had just left after administrating the last rights. Daniels was pacing his cell when the door opened, and in walked Mrs. Daniels escorted by a guard.

Prison rules forbid visitors from entering an inmate's cell. For weeks, while visiting her son, Mrs. Daniels sat in a chair just outside of his cell. This day was different. Mr. Miller unlocked the door to Daniel's cell and allowed her to walk inside. He locked the door behind her, winked, and left the room.

Without saying a word, she put her arms around her son and held him tight. She buried her tear-soaked face into his breast as she had done with her pillow every night. After several moments, she pulled away wiping her face with a hankie. She dropped into a chair while Daniels sat on the edge of his bed.

"How have you been, Son?" she asked. "Are they treating you okay?"

"I'm doing okay."

"Why did that guard let me in here? I thought they had some kind of rule against it."

"Mr. Miller has been good to me. Besides, he's near retirement, so he doesn't care much about prison rules," said Daniels wiping a tear from his cheek.

"I can't believe this is happening."

"I know Ma."

"I can't believe how fast the time went by."

Daniels said nothing. He reached out and took his mother's hand.

Mrs. Daniels forced a smile through the tears. "I remember when you were a child. You would fall down and scrape your knees. Mama would fix you up and away you'd go back outside. Seemed like it wasn't but a few minutes later you'd be back with some other kind of problem."

"Maybe that was my problem. Maybe I was a mama's boy."

She smiled. "No, Son. I can assure you that you weren't a mama's boy."

There was a long pause.

"I don't know what to say," she said, tears running down her face.

Daniels tightly gripped her hand and smothered it with his other one. "I know, Ma."

There was another long pause.

"I wish I had a lot of things to do over," she said. "Maybe if I had been a better mother…"

"Don't do this to yourself, Mom. You were a great mother and don't forget it," he said with conviction.

"I don't know."

"This has nothing to do with you," he said. "I know how you get some things stuck in your head. Don't let this idea be one of them."

"I'm not coming tomorrow, Son," she blurted. "I couldn't bear to see you tomorrow. It wouldn't be right for a mother to see her son on a day such as that. I hope you understand."

"I understand," he said.

"Your father didn't want to come tonight. It's been so hard on him. He's tried so hard to be brave and not show his emotions." She paused. "He sends his love and… he sends his love and a goodbye." She bowed her head and wept.

Daniels bowed his head as the tears gushed down his face.

It was minutes later before they both regained their composure.

"I was remembering that Christmas when Pop bought me that BB gun. That was my favorite Christmas."

He went out and borrowed money to buy us presents that year. It was the last time he did that since he was paying for it up until fall of the next year."

"I'm pretty sure that BB gun is still at home in my closet."

"Sorry, Son, but I threw it out years ago. Neither your father nor me had much use for guns around the house."

"I remember picking off a black bird in that walnut tree in the backyard. My God, was Pop ever mad when he found out. Took away my gun for a month. Worse than that, he made me bury the little fellow in the backyard. Pop was teaching me something there. Wish I had listened."

"I hope you know that just because your father isn't here, doesn't mean he doesn't love you."

"I know, Mom."

"I think he wants to remember you as that kid with the BB gun."

Daniels wiped his eyes and scooted closer to his mother. "I'm scared, Mom," he said his lips quivering.

Mrs. Daniels got out of her chair and sat next to her son. She wrapped him in her arms and held him tightly. "Oh, God, I'm going to miss you so much."

"Please remember, Mom, that I love you."

"I love you too, Son."

For the next several minutes, they remained locked in an embrace. For the rest of her life, that last embrace with her son would haunt her very soul. She wanted to remember her son as he was that day, but the memory hurt too much.

Suddenly, she broke away and got to her feet. "I have to go, Son. Call the guard for me, please."

He stood and called for Mr. Miller. Almost immediately, the steel door opened, and the gray-haired man stepped inside. He unlocked the door to Daniel's cell, swung it open and turned his back to the two people standing just ten feet away.

Mrs. Daniels took two steps towards the open door, turned and wrapped her arms around her son.

"Goodbye, Son," she said. "God be with you."

"Goodbye, Mom," he said, his voice crackling. "Always remember that you were a good mother."

She covered her face with her hankie, turned and walked away.

Chapter Twenty One

It was January 3, 1949, the day proclaimed by a panel of judges to be the last day on earth for Robert Murl Daniels. The morning dawned with dark, ominous clouds that seemed to touch the ground. Wisps of snow filled the air giving promise of another cold winter day.

A key rattled in a steel door, and a guard carrying a tray of food entered. Daniels was sitting on the edge of his bed with his head in his hands.

"Good morning, Mr. Daniels," said the guard sliding the tray into the cell.

"Morning, Mr. Miller," Daniels muttered.

"Get any sleep?"

"Not a wink."

"That's good."

"Why do you say that?"

"Dulls the senses," said Miller. "You're less aware of what's going on."

Daniels glanced at the tray. "I don't think I can eat a bite. I'll just throw it back up."

"Well, I'll just leave it there just in case you get hungry."

Daniels sat up and turned to the guard. "What's it like. Mr. Miller?"

"What's what like?"

"You know…"

"Oh, I don't want to talk about it."

"It's okay, Mr. Miller. Just tell me what you know."

"Well, I don't know much about what goes on. All I know is that they'll come to get you sometime late this afternoon shortly after you have your last meal. They're going to take you over to a little building called the death house. What goes on in there, I can only guess."

"Surely you must have heard."

"Not interested. No, siree. Never even been inside that place."

"I take it you don't believe in the death penalty."

"No opinion, one way or the other. I just don't want any part of the execution of a man."

Daniels put his head in his hands. "I tell you it's got me so scared I'm pissing my pants." He looked up at Miller. "I got to know. Is it fast and painless?"

"You don't want to know."

"So you do know what happens. Somebody told you, didn't they?"

"Let's just say it's over with in less than ten minutes."

"Ten minutes! You mean to tell me I'm going to burn in that thing for ten minutes. How many volts do they use?"

"I don't know."

"Yes, you do. Now tell me how many?"

"Someone said that it's 2,000 volts."

"They're going to pass 2,000 volts through my body, and it will take ten minutes to kill me! Oh, good Lord help me. Think of the pain that I will have to endure."

"Actually, I heard there is no pain involved. The first jolt knocks you out. You don't feel a thing."

Daniels slowly shook his head. "I'd like to believe that. Besides, how would anybody know?"

"Sorry, Mr. Daniels," said Miller and slowly walked out of the room.

It was a little after four in the afternoon when he ate his last meal. As was the tradition, he was allowed to have anything he wanted. He had fried oysters, fried chicken, chili con carne, potatoes, limburger cheese spread, bread, butter, coffee, grape juice, orange juice, vanilla ice cream with chocolate syrup, and chocolate cake.

He originally extended an invitation to reporters to come and watch him eat his last meal but declined to see newsmen during his final day of life. When he finished his meal, he was taken back to his cell on death row to await the trip to the death chamber.

Daniels collapsed on the edge of his bed. His legs shook so badly he could hardly stand. His hands quivered as if he were having convulsions. He leaned back on the bed and fell asleep.

At 5:45, two guards entered his cell and helped him get to his feet. They shackled his hands and feet and led him out of the room. They escorted him down hallways and through locked doors until they were outside in the cold January air. It was a short walk to the death chamber, but Daniels shivered, convulsively, all the way.

As they reached the door to the death chamber, Daniels' legs buckled. One of the guards reached out and helped him to walk the last few feet. At 6:00, they locked him in the death cell. The time for his execution had been set for 8:00. Robert Daniels had only two hours to live.

An hour later, the door opened. Daniels jumped. It was Father Lucier, the penitentiary Catholic chaplain. He sat next to Daniels and began to slowly read from the Bible. By then, Daniels was dazed and didn't hear a word he muttered.

At 7:55, Warden Alvis, three physicians, the executioner, and 17 witnesses filed into a small room. They crowded around the walls facing a wooden chair perched on a small platform. The warden tapped twice on a door. The door opened, and the priest slowly walked into the room softly reciting the Lord's Prayer over and over. Then Daniels appeared, his eyes closed and his head bowed. He was praying aloud with the priest. The two guards supported him as he walked to the chair.

With some degree of effort, Daniels stepped upon the platform, and with help from the guards eased into the chair. By then, his mutterings of the Lord's Prayer were indiscernible, punctuated with quiet sobs.

Daniels grew silent as two guards began to strap him in. Straps were fastened around his wrists, his forearms and ankles. As they positioned his legs into the metal clamps, one of the guards dipped a rag into a bucket of saltwater and soaked the clamp and leg area. The other guard then tightened the clamp firmly around Daniel's legs.

One of the guards once again dipped the rag into the brine and swabbed the electrodes. Daniels flinched as he attached them to his head. The guard paused and then leaned over to whisper into Daniels' ear. He stood erect and then lowered a black mask over his head. He and the other guard and Father Lucier stepped back from the chair. Daniels dug his fingernails into the handles of the chair. Silence filled the room as all eyes turned to the warden. Some of the witnesses quietly wept, while others turned away.

The warden nodded to the executioner. He reached to the wall and pulled a large handle. A blue light that was on the wall behind Daniels went off, and a red one flashed on.

Daniels' body lurched upward tearing at the straps. His body remained rigid, the tendons and veins of his neck and legs standing out against the reddening flesh.

Father Lucier finished the Lord's Prayer alone.

As the powerful current passed through his body, his fists remained clenched and resting on the arms of the chair. The hum of the generator became quiet, and the red light was replaced by the blue one. His body slumped deep into the chair. Fifteen seconds had passed. Many of the witnesses who had looked away, now slowly and cautiously turned back to the macabre scene.

After the passage of another fifteen seconds, the blue light gave way to the red, and Daniels' body again lunged against the confining straps. The powerful jolt of electricity crackled and snapped as it seared through his body. Faint wisps of smoke rose from the electrode around his leg swirling between his knees and seeped through the cotton mask that covered his head.

As the lights again changed, the reddened flesh about his chest and throat turned to a bluish-black color. His head was thrown back, and once again he slumped into the chair, this time motionless. The business of killing was silent now. The only sound was the quiet weeping of witnesses.

A prison doctor approached Daniels. He carefully pulled back his shirt revealing his blackened chest. For two minutes, he probed with his stethoscope searching for any signs of life. He stepped aside, and another doctor made his examination. He turned to the spectators and said, "Sufficient electricity has passed through the body of Robert Murl Daniels to have caused death at 8:09 p.m."

The warden and the witnesses filed out of the room. Two guards removed the remains from the chair and took them to a waiting hearse.

The warden was to inform the governor that Daniels had been executed. He dialed a number then spoke just five words. "Bob? Warden. Death, 8:09. Goodnight."

THE END

Postscript

In the summer of 2008, I set out to find Russell Niebel, the sole surviving member of the family. It had been sixty years nearly to the day since his father, John, his mother, Nolana and his sister, Phyllis were brutally murdered in a cornfield off Fleming Falls Road. I found eighty-three year old, Russ Niebel working in a small television and radio repair shop on Park Avenue.

At the time of the murders in 1948, Mr. Niebel was in Chicago attending a television and radio repair school. He had nearly completed a two-year program and was preparing for graduation.

It was his brother, Loyal Niebel, who had suggested that he enter the field of TV repair. At the end of World War II, they both returned home from the Navy and began searching for work. Loyal had been trained as an electronics technician and strongly advised his brother to enter that field. In spite of the fact that neither TV's nor TV broadcasting stations existed during the late forties, Russell packed up his belongings and moved to Chicago to learn how to repair televisions. Nearly eighteen months later and just six months shy of graduation, Russell returned to Mansfield, Ohio to bury three members of his family. He was hired by Mansfield Radio and TV in 1948 and is still working there today.

I found Mr. Niebel in the backroom of his shop. I introduced myself, and he asked me to sit down. He was a short, stocky man who appeared to be in great physical condition. He was well groomed and wore a warm and friendly smile.

I sensed from the very beginning of our meeting there was a certain amount of reluctance on his part to talk with me. I guessed that he was afraid I would ask questions about the tragic events of July, 1948. He soon began to relax when he realized I was only interested in the lives of his family and not their deaths.

I opened my notebook and clicked my pen. "Tell me about Phyllis," I said.

"She was the sweetest and kindest person I ever met," he said without hesitation.

"She taught Sunday school, didn't she?" I asked.

"Yes, she did," said Mr. Niebel. "And I was told that she was very good at it."

"I read somewhere that she was about to celebrate her twenty-first birthday."

"Mom and Dad were making plans," he said. "They had already contacted many of her friends."

"Did she have many dates?"

"I remember that she dated many boys while in high school and after she graduated as well. She had a particular friend that summer. I don't remember his name, but I know they were quite serious about each other."

"Many have said that the loss of Phyllis was incredibly heartbreaking," I said. "Even Daniels had regrets. After everything I've read and heard about her, I must say she must have been quite a young woman."

"That she was," he said nodding his head.

"Tell me about your father," I said with an upbeat voice. "I read that he was a very strong man with a righteous character."

"He was all of that and more," said Mr. Niebel. "He was well liked and highly respected by not only the prison officials but the prisoners as well. You know, he was in charge of the entire prison farm including the gardens and the livestock. To check on the different operations of the farm, I remember he used a horse and buggy which was a bit unusual for the times. For some reason, I remember his horse's name was Rex. Why I would remember something like that is beyond me."

"Your mother's name was Nolana," I said. "Tell me what she was like."

"There was always laughter in the house when my mother was there. She was incredibly kind and loved to have fun. She was a deeply religious woman and read from the Bible every chance she got. I never heard her or my father say a bad word except for one time. I don't remember what the occasion was, but I remember she used the word, 'shit.' What a shock that was."

"I believe I heard from a friend of the family that she was a part of a women's group."

"Actually, she was the one who started the group of women they called the Willing Club. They made quilts and canned fruits and vegetables to give to poor people. It was a worthy idea, but if the truth be known, I think it was just an excuse to get together and gossip."

"I've driven by the house that you lived in. From the pictures I've seen in the newspapers from 1948, it hasn't changed a bit. It looks the same as it did sixty years ago."

Mr. Niebel's face sobered. "I've never been back to that house since it happened. I thought about it but never did it. As far as that goes, I've never read anything about what happened. In all these years, I've never had a nightmare, and I'm not starting now."

"Your house is the only one on that road. It stands there alone among small factories and commercial buildings. Was that the way it looked in 1948?"

"Back then the road was called Main Street, and it was just an ordinary residential street. Houses like ours lined both sides of the street with a small party store just down the road."

"Seems strange, Mr. Niebel, that they tore all those houses down but yours. Any idea why?"

"I have no idea."

"If you don't mind my asking, whatever happened to your brother, Loyal?"

"Loyal died of MS back in 1966."

"From what I read, he must have been a good brother to you."

"He was the best," said Mr. Niebel with a warm, almost nostalgic smile. "If it hadn't been for him, I don't know what I would have done. He took care of all the details. I had a great admiration and respect for his strength."

As I got ready to leave, Mr. Niebel asked me a question that gave me pause. He asked me if I had decided on a name for the book. At the time, I had a working title of COLD-BLOODED MURDER. That title seemed a bit insensitive if not sensational, so I told him that I had not decided on a title as yet. I did not mean to lie to the man, but I couldn't believe that he would find any comfort in hearing those words.

Several weeks later, I met with Mr. Niebel again. I asked him questions about his family, and he cordially answered them. He seemed much more relaxed this time. I'm sure he was convinced that I would not ask any sensitive or painful questions. He is a wonderful man, and I hope to someday see him again.

***

In an effort to recreate the tragic events that led to the Niebel murders, we traveled to Fleming Falls Road and soon found the cornfield where they were taken that night. However, we could only guess where the exact spot was located. With a considerable amount of good luck, we were able to find a woman who lived on Fleming Falls Road back in 1948. She showed us the spot where the three Niebels were murdered. It gave me an eerie feeling to stand on that part of the cornfield. I had dealt with haunts from the past in my life but nothing so vividly disturbing.

Interestingly enough, if those same murders had taken place today and the bodies left in a cornfield, it's highly unlikely they would have been discovered so soon. In those days, farmers planted corn in neat, straight rows with stalks nearly a foot apart. If positioned correctly, one could see a great distance into a cornfield. Today's farmers have a high regard for the yield produced by a field. To that end, they plant corn so that the stalks are clustered together producing a yield many times greater than years ago. Nothing within the field can be seen beyond the outer row of corn. Three bodies ten feet into the field would not have been discovered by the casual passerby.

July 21, 2008, marked the sixtieth year since the Niebel murders. On that date, my wife and I stopped by the Mansfield Cemetery. It was a winding, single lane road that led us to the Niebel plots. With flowers in hand, we climbed the small hill and stopped in front of a large stone. The name, NIEBEL, was boldly etched on the front of the stone and beneath it was inscribed, "Rest Cometh With The Night." At the time, I thought what a peculiar phrase for a tombstone, and yet it seemed somehow appropriate and even honorable for the three fallen family members. The three plots were laid out side-by-side with Loyal's grave nearby.

I turned my attention away from the graves. From my vantage point on the side of that small hill, I could see a good portion of the cemetery. I tried to imagine the somber proceedings sixty years ago with Reverend Hagelbarger trying desperately to console and ease the pain of the surviving family members. He stood there looking out across a sea of people probably the largest crowd he had ever addressed and said, "Lord to whom shall we go? Thou hast words of eternal life."

I humbly dedicate this book to the memory of John Niebel, Nolana, Phyllis, and Loyal. I especially dedicate this book to Russell Niebel for all of his help. He is truly a wonderful man.

The Ohio State Reformatory

The Ohio State Reformatory has been a landmark in this part of Ohio for over a century.

The reformatory boasts two features that make it famous throughout the United States. The first claim to fame is the number of movies shot within its walls which include The *Shawshank Redemption* and *Air Force One* among others. The second feature of the Ohio State Reformatory that has made it famous is that it is quite simply haunted.

It is considered by many to be in the top ten of the most haunted places in America. Not only has the Travel Channel's

Ghost Adventures visited the reformatory; it has been explored twice by Syfy channel's Ghost Hunters show. It has also been featured on Fox Family Channel's Real Scary Stories, Scariest Places on Earth, and Most Terrifying Places in America.

It opened its doors in 1896 to its first 150 young offenders. The doors to the prison closed in 1990 after housing over 155,000 men. Since then it has remained intact by the help of donations and volunteers by the hundreds. Guided tours are conducted throughout the summer months but come to an end in September due to the fact there is no heat in the building.

Probably one of the most talked about and famous features of the reformatory are the all night, self-guided tours offered during the summer months. One night each month, a small group of about thirty people are locked inside the walls of the reformatory. They are given a quick tour of the hotspots, promised a pizza dinner at around midnight and then are locked inside the walls until morning. During the night, anyone can leave if it should get too much for them, but they are locked out for the rest of the night and cannot return.

A few years back, a friend of mine, his wife and another couple spent the night in the reformatory. They took the quick tour and after being locked in for the night, they decided to sit down in a hallway and quietly observe their surroundings. He said that in a very short time, they witnessed the image of a man peeking around the corner of a window. After a few moments, his head would disappear behind the wall then moments later reappear. Since they were on the second floor, they made the assumption he was standing on a ledge of some sort. This went on for quite some time, and after trying desperately to communicate with the individual, they decided to walk over to the window. As they peered out the window, they were shocked to see that there was no ledge, floor or anything else that anyone could have stood on.

I've often wondered if the spirits of John West and Robert Daniels have ever visited the reformatory. After all, they were incarcerated within its walls for several years. I had heard rumors of people hearing the voice of Robert Daniels somewhere around the superintendent's office. So, I contacted officials of the reformatory, and they told me that nobody had ever had any contact with the spirits of either John West or Robert Daniels.

Six miles East of Van Wert, Ohio stands Ohio State Historical Marker 2-81. It is located at the intersection of Rt. 224 and Rt. 637. The front of the marker reads: Killing Spree Ends Here in

1948." I just made the journey to the other side of Ohio to visit the spot where the two week reign of terror ended. It is located at the crossroads of two state routes in the middle of Ohio cornfields. It is a small fenced in area with a granite seat in front of the marker.

I would have hoped that this would be the end of my obsession, but there is one last thing for me to do. I must find out where John West and Robert Daniels are buried. Maybe then I can put this whole story to rest.

The Niebels' house as it looks today and back in 1948

The historical marker at Rt. 224 and Rt. 637

About the Author

In 1996 with a lifelong dream of being a writer, Scott Fields started writing short stories. Within the two years, he had four  stories published. Since then, his first novel, *All Those Years Ago*, was published, and in the fall of 2004, his second novel, *A Summer Harvest*, was released. His third novel, *The Road Back Home*, was published in the fall of 2007 by Charles River Press, and his fourth novel, *Last Days of Summer*, was released by Whiskey Creek Press. *Summer Heat*, his fifth novel, was published in May 2012 by Outer Banks Publishing Group.

Scott and his wife, Deb, live in Mansfield, Ohio.

Also by Scott Fields

Summer Heat - A hot summer, a sultry town flirt whose husband was away and an opportunity she had never faced. What followed was a series of sordid events involving murder, deceit, betrayal and the conviction of an innocent man in this erotic novel.

Available in fine book stores everywhere and as an ebook on Kindle, iBooks, Barnes & Noble, Kobo and other ebook retailers.

15984740R00162

Made in the USA
Charleston, SC
29 November 2012